TOR BOOKS BY POUL ANDERSON

Alight in the Void
The Armies of Elfland
The Boat of a Million Years
The Dancer from Atlantis
The Day of Their Return
Explorations
Harvest of Stars
Harvest the Fire
Hoka! *(with Gordon R. Dickson)*
Kinship with the Stars
A Knight of Ghosts and Shadows
The Long Night
The Longest Voyage
Maurai and Kith
A Midsummer Tempest
No Truce with Kings
Past Times
The Saturn Game
The Shield of Time
The Stars Are Also Fire
Tales of the Flying Mountains
The Time Patrol
There Will Be Time

POUL ANDERSON

HARVEST THE FIRE

TOR ®

A TOM DOHERTY ASSOCIATES BOOK
NEW YORK

This is a work of fiction. All the characters and events portrayed in this book are either products of the author's imagination or are used fictitiously.

HARVEST THE FIRE

Cover art by Vincent Di Fate

Edited by David G. Hartwell

A Tor Book
Published by Tom Doherty Associates, Inc.
175 Fifth Avenue
New York, NY 10010

Tor Books on the World Wide Web:
http://www.tor.com

Tor® is a registered trademark of Tom Doherty Associates, Inc.

ISBN: 0-812-55375-6
Library of Congress Card Catalog Number: 95-30304

First Tor edition: October 1995
First mass market edition: November 1997

Printed in the United States of America

0 9 8 7 6 5 4 3 2 1

To
Ted Chichak,
who made this one possible.

HARVEST THE FIRE

PROLOGUE

_____

_____

_____

Once in his drifting to and fro across Earth, Jesse Nicol found a quivira left over from olden times. It was in a hotel that stood alone, grounds walled on three sides by rain forest, above Iguazú Falls. From the terrace he looked across a lawn to the verge of an abyss. He barely glimpsed the top of one cataract, but upflung mist smoked white into heaven and the roar, though muted by distance, passed into his bones.

Strange, he thought, that anyone here had ever wanted to retreat straight into a dreamworld. When he remarked on it, the manager told him that the raw magnificence they came to see had put some guests into a mood for a wild experience, wherefore this facility had been installed to oblige them.

Nowadays, of course, the place was nearly deserted. Most people who might feel curious about the cascades and the surrounding wilderness preserve were content to stay home and let their vivifers give them multisense-recorded tours. Most rooms stood shut off and empty. Only maintainors purred about on their programmed rounds, holding subtropical air and nature at bay, keeping the building in good repair, for it was a historical relic and did still draw occasional visitors.

Having walked the trails, Nicol returned full of what he beheld. As he washed, changed clothes, and ate alone in the big dining room, served by a silent robot, the waters querned in his spirit, an elemental force. Even on this tamed and machine-teeming planet, he had seen the universe at work. It spoke to him of mightiness and mysteries, meanings beyond words for which he nonetheless longed to find words, evoking the awe in others through lifetime after lifetime to come.

He might as well have tried to sculpture the mists. Nothing would take form; everything slipped through his grasp, save for bare and hueless lumps of phrase that he cast from him in an almost physical spasm.

Exultation drained away. Disgust and despair thickened in his gullet. Again he was failing. Why, why, why? Shakespeare could have drawn a poem out of the thunders to shake the soul *(Blow, winds, and crack your cheeks! rage! blow!)*, or Kipling *(Wrecks of our wrath dropped reeling down as we fought and we spurned and we strove.)*, or Borges *(Quien lo mira lo ve por primera vez—)*, or hundreds more across the ages. What crippled him? He could not so much as give voice to his own powerlessness. Hopkins had done it, in the ancestral language that Nicol had ransacked over and over—

> Birds build—but not I build; no, but strain,
> Time's eunuch, and not breed one word that wakes.
> Mine, O thou lord of life, send my roots rain.

despite also creating "Pied Beauty" and "The Windhover."

Nicol knew he had a gift. He felt it. Genome analysis in his infancy had shown the potential. He didn't suppose he could have become a new Homer, but surely he could make something worth remembering.

He never had. At best, his verses climbed a little above banality. The knowledge became a corrosion in him, brewing rage that too often spat itself at the closest random object.

He would not let it, not today, when he had just gloried in his smallness and mortality. He called for a third glass of wine and, with an effort, paid heed to aroma and savor. The glow already in his blood strengthened. After a while his thoughts flowed calmly, more ironic than bitter.

The time is out of joint—Yes, old Will had said it, as he said all else. All else human, anyway. His imagination had not encompassed the cybercosm. How could it have? Nicol did not understand today's world either. What merely organic creature ever would? This era had its virtues, doubtless more people were happy than anywhen else in history, but it was not an era to inspire poets. And no artist works in isolation. However abstract or romantic, art of any kind—not diversion or decoration, but that

which lays hold of the soul and will not let go—springs
from the realities around it.

Precedents were abundant, moments of radiancy out-
shining everything that happened for generations earlier
and generations afterward, Amarnan, Periclean, Tang,
Elizabethan . . . and the dull times, the dim times, when
the hack and the academic reigned, when nobody took
fire because there was no fire, times whose work soon lay
forgotten, unless eventually a scholar exhumed a bit of it
for curiosity's sake.

Nicol had done that now and then, in a desultory, ama-
teur fashion. He had puzzled over the phenomenon,
aware that he was by no means the first. Why this jagged
distribution of greatness? The incidence of innate abilities
could scarcely vary that much. The social situation, the
Zeitgeist—were such phrases anything but noises? Usually
he had dismissed his speculations with a sneer and a
curse.

This evening, however, sitting solitary at the table, he
found them astir again, and half in focus. (The scrambled
metaphors provoked a wry grin.) A line from Jorge Luis
Borges crossed his mind. Well, that man had been among
the rare exceptions to the rule. Consider: The first half of
the twentieth century was a supernova in literature as well
as in science and technology. After about 1950, while
knowledge of the cosmos and achievement within it
waxed on and on, creativity in the traditional arts gut-
tered close to extinction. What makers from that time still
spoke to Nicol about had basically been completing work
they began earlier—aside from Borges and a very few others.

True, he was born in—1899, was it?—and much of his writing appeared before the First Global War. Yet he went on from triumph to triumph until the end of a life rather long for those days. *El oro de los tigros* was published in the last third of the twentieth century.

How could that be?

Impulse grabbed. Here Nicol was, in Borges's Argentine, with a full-capability quivira on hand and enough credit to pay for whatever special service would be required. Why not? He might, he just might, learn something that would help him. At the least, instead of futilely brooding, he ought to get some hours worthy of the past several.

He sought out the manager, who exclaimed in surprise, "You wish to use it, señor? Why, may I ask? Hardly anyone goes to a quivira any more, when dreamboxes are everywhere."

"I know," said Nicol. "But a dreambox can only draw on the standard programs."

"The selection is huge, señor. I do not know how many millions of different milieus and situations you can choose from."

"Still, I suspect they don't contain exactly what I want. A quivira is equipped to work with the cybercosm and produce a new one. Don't worry, this is nothing perverse." Nicol laughed. "I agree, it's probably impossible to invent anything along those lines that isn't already available. Basically, I want to meet a man who died hundreds of years ago."

That was a common desire, and simulations of historic figures were activated every day in dreamboxes around

the world. Nicol simply doubted that Borges was among them. How many today had heard of, let alone read, him? Quite apart from changes in language, those subtle, elegiac lines were altogether alien to an age wherein the boundaries he knew, between nature and artifice, organic and inorganic, life and death, were no more.

Nicol felt alien too.

The manager shrugged, led him down hushed corridors, and unsecured a door for him. The suite beyond was heavy with antique elegance. Quiviras in their heyday were not exclusively resorts for pseudo-events; they were small centers for real-time relaxation and indulgence, for discreet rendezvous and confidential talk. Nicol believed that more than the development of inexpensive, easily operated equipment had made them obsolete. Societies themselves had mutated.

He settled down at the main control board. His childhood in space had left him with computer skills superior to the average, and the unit helped him when he encountered problems. Soon he was in touch with a high-order sophotect. No, it informed him, a Borges program did not exist. Yes, one could be prepared. The charge would be stiff, especially since he wanted the job done quickly—which meant mobilizing considerable resources, to scan the databases of the world and from their information synthesize a personality and setting, all in about an hour—but it was in the range of what he could afford. Roaming in modest style, he spent his citizen's credit less fast than it was issued him.

Was the machine mind giving him a break because it was interested in the project and in seeing what would happen?

Waiting for his excursion to be ready, he went to his room and took a detoxer. Alcohol purged from his system, he came back alert and eager. The manager had summoned a live attendant who, hastily briefed, helped him disrobe, fitted the helmet to his head and the connections to his skin, and led him into the bath. He felt a trifle irritated; a modern dreambox didn't require a second party. Mastering the emotion, he lay down in the tank. The fluid rose around him, took on his mean density and skin temperature, became a sensationless womb where he floated blind and deaf. The circuits began sending their gentle pulses into his brain and he slipped away toward sleep.

To sleep, perchance to dream— But no, he thought, rehearsing the obvious to himself as people may when wakefulness is departing. Not true sleep, not passive and chaotic dreaming. The program was interactive. Within its broad limits, it would respond to whatever he did and said in his mind like the real world and real persons responding to his material body. Not in real time, of course; in an hour by the clock he might well experience several subjective hours. Afterward they would be in his memory exactly the same as all others, nothing but logic to tell him these events had been imaginary.

Were they? Their effects on his neurons would be no different. And how real is a poem or a snatch of music?

Down and down.

Out, into bright sunshine on an enormously broad and racketing street.

First he looked at himself. He wore the awkward, uncomfortable garb of the twentieth century, jacket over a shirt and necktie dangling under his throat. Buenos Aires in this period was a dressy city. The air was mild, but foul with the fumes of internal-combustion cars. They crowded the pavement between high, handsome buildings, as pedestrians did the walkways alongside. Folk generally seemed prosperous and cheerful.

Nicol wondered about that. The program immediately informed him. It felt as if he were recalling material he had personally studied. Yes, Argentina in Borges's last years went through some savage times. However, he had lived to see a fair measure of democracy established and a new hopefulness. Probably the program was showing this symbolically, Nicol decided. The cybercosm wouldn't simulate more than his purpose required. This was not the Avenida 9 de Julio on which he stood; these were not human beings around him; it was all a shadow show intended only to give him an idea of the environment. If he strayed off a straight course to his goal, he would come into empty streets and then into a blankness from which he would abruptly rouse in his tank.

A shiver passed through him. He almost wished he had not elected to remain aware that this was in fact a pseudo-world.

Concrete hard beneath his feet, chemical reek in his nostrils, rumble and clatter and voices in his ears, gave reassurance. He strode ahead.

At the imposing building on Calle México that housed the Central Library, he met no difficulty. He spoke the contemporary language fluently, or had the illusion he did, which amounted to the same thing. A three-dimensional shadow said he was expected and conducted him to the director. That post was basically honorary, but when

Borges held it he had fallen into the habit of using the office in the mornings, dictating stories and poems, before going home to work with his translator into Anglo—into English. Nicol's heart fluttered as he was ushered in. The door closed softly at his back.

The old blind man behind the desk heard and rose, offering his hand, as courteous as every true aristocrat. A smile brought the plain, somewhat heavy face totally alive. "Welcome," he bade. "It is always a pleasure to meet an American. I have never had times more marvelous, or been more kindly treated, than in your country. Please be seated. Shall I ring for coffee?"

He resumed his own chair, still smiling, among the books he had so loved, now forever closed to his eyes. As the minutes passed, as he talked warmly, wittily, wisely, it grew more and more hard for Nicol to comprehend that he was not in the presence of the mortal Jorge Luis Borges.

What difference, anyhow? When the cybercosm wrote this program, it took into account everything recorded about the man, his life, friends, loves, environs and their history, above all his works. The program behaved, it re-acted and spoke to Nicol's mind, just as if it had in fact written *Ficciones* and *Elogio de la sombra* and—and it could not write what else Borges wrote after this date, but how vividly it talked, gestured, radiated intellect and goodwill.

Among its data was the pseudo-fact that Nicol was a young man from that nation known as the United States of America, recommended to Borges by an associate he had had while at Harvard University. The program seemed relieved that the visitor wanted less to discuss the works as such than the enigma of creativity, its well-springs, what nourished and what withered it.

No, Nicol thought, forget that this is only an engineered dream, an artifact of the cybercosm interacting with what goes on in my brain. To all momentary intents and purposes, I am here and now with *him*. Let me gather as much as I can of his insights.

The conversation stayed with him for the rest of his days, but he never mentioned it to anyone else. It was his private possession, a part of his inmost self. On that account, it often struck more deeply than he could admit. Borges would have had no way of knowing what hurt the other or seeing it on him.

"—the symbols of a society, do they hold its soul within them? No New England churchyard, nor Arlington Cemetery, stands in your mind for quite what La Recoleta does in mine. I think that is a major reason we cannot foretell the future. We can perhaps guess at its technology, a little, and a little less at how that technology will touch daily life, but we cannot know what it will mean."

Cold lightning went up Nicol's spine. "Maybe you could, sir," burst from him.

"I? Hardly."

"You . . . you've dealt with strangeness, better than anyone else, I think, and the future is very strange. You might see the heart of it, the thing that can't be spoken but that everything is about."

Borges raised his brows. "I do not believe so. I would not have lived in it. In any case, first we require a history of that which has not yet happened."

"Allow me, please allow me," Nicol said desperately. "A whim, a wild fancy, whatever you like, but, but important to me. Imagine I'm a time traveler come back, who can tell you that history, tell you what it's like up there. Then tell me what you might write if that was your period."

Borges sat silent for a span, until he answered low, "You overestimate me, I fear. I have attempted nothing as fanciful as this. But I hear that it matters to you. Therefore, say on, because you are my guest."

Nicol drew breath and plunged.

Afterward he recalled that part of the day the least clearly. He had no plan, no ordered arrangement of facts to present. At first he floundered about, scrambling everything together, spaceflight, nanotechnology, psychonetics, wars, revolutions, new species of beast and man, helter-skelter from his lips. But after a while Borges said, "This is very interesting. You seem to have invented a world as complete as Tolkien's. Let us explore it." He began to ask questions. And things to come took shape for the blind man.

Or so the illusion went. What the words might have signified to the living Borges, Nicol could never know. Anything at all, other than an elaborate fantasy? Trying to guess, he stepped mentally aside from what he had related and looked at it for a second as objectively as he was able.

Humans did not get into space to stay until the cost of launch was brought down to a reasonable figure. This was done largely by a private corporation, Fireball Enter-

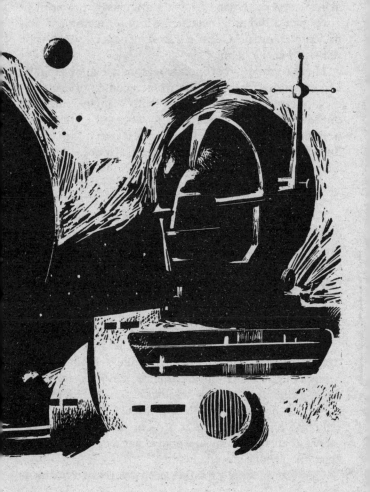

prises, which for a long while thereafter took the lead in activity beyond Earth. Growing immensely powerful, it nevertheless did not "degenerate into a government," as its founder Anson Guthrie was wont to say, because he remained at the helm.

There were sound economic reasons for colonizing the Moon, but it turned out that women could not bring babies to term in the low gravity. Genetic engineering produced the race of Lunarians, to whom the conditions were natural. What nobody expected was that they would differ even more in temperament than in body from the Terran stock that gave rise to them. As their first generations matured, friction worsened between the two species.

The age was cruel as well as brilliant. Not only did genetic engineering bring forth many useful new life-forms, the experiments of certain governments led to several other human breeds, who became pathetic misfits. A byproduct of this research were the Keiki Moana, intelligent monk seals, whom Fireball finally took under its protection. All living things that were the result of such technology were known as metamorphs.

Dazzling developments occurred also in cybernetics. Robots of every kind became versatile and ubiquitous. Many could learn from experience, carry on conversations, make decisions, or otherwise behave like people. However, they remained sharply limited. No matter how elaborate its program, what a robot essentially did was carry out an algorithm. The goal of a truly conscious artificial intelligence stayed elusive.

This was in spite of rather early success with downloads. By nanotechnic and quantum mechanical means, a nervous system could be scanned virtually molecule by molecule. The basic patterns of memory and personality could then be mapped into a program for a neural network of complexity comparable to the brain's. In effect, a download was a copy of a person's mind, equipped with sensors and a speaker, capable of hookup to a machine body. Fireball retained its integrity because Guthrie lived long enough to undergo the process before his death. His download continued in charge. Few persons ever opted for such a ghost-existence, and of those, hardly any chose to carry it on for long. Download Guthrie had sufficient of his original's vigor and interest in life to do so.

The United Nations and many countries collapsed in war and civil breakdown. A stronger World Federation rose out of the ruins, but during the hiatus a unique civilization had had a chance to develop among the Lunarians, and at length they won their independence. Theirs became a nation without a formal government, dominated rather than ruled by the families of the Selenarchs. It colonized widely through the Asteroid Belt, the moons of the giant planets, and Mars. Politicians and bureaucrats on Earth felt uneasy about those "anarchists" running loose, refusing membership in the Federation.

New crises came to a head on the mother world. At last Fireball had no choice but to commit what amounted to an act of war, in alliance with the Selenarch Rinndalir and his associates. The reaction to this meant the doom of both. Guthrie negotiated and bought time while he made his preparations. Fireball had already sent exploratory probes to the nearest neighbor star, Alpha Centauri, which had one marginally habitable planet and numerous asteroids. By trading off the company's assets, he got the means to make the tremendous journey there with a handful of Terran and Lunarian dissidents. Everybody knew that in a thousand years the planet, Demeter, would collide with another. But those thousand years could be lived in, and perhaps during them the descendants of the colonists would find a means of surviving.

The Federation brought Luna forcibly back into itself, as a member republic complete with democratic institutions that ill suited Lunarians. At first, being in the large majority, they could often evade or ignore the new laws. But then the Federation government moved the abandoned L-5 colony, a big artificial satellite of Earth, into a low Lunar orbit, stabilized by solar sails—the Habitat. Given the artificial gravity engendered by its spin, Terrans could reproduce in easy reach of the Moon, moving there to stay when their children were old enough. Before long they outnumbered and outvoted the Lunarians.

Another unhappy society was the Lahui Kuikawa, which had evolved among the Keiki Moana and their human partners. Cramped and restricted on a Hawaiian reservation, they at last—incidentally to a larger intrigue—got a mid-Pacific island and its surrounding waters for their own, where they could live with scant outside interference. Other cultures, some still more curious, were quietly developing around the planet.

This happened well after the first true artificial intelligence, the first sophotect, had come into being. Once they had a nonalgorithmic model of consciousness, researchers became able to create it. Given the resources at its disposal, the sophotectic mind rapidly outpaced the organic. It was never divided among distinct personalities. Those could exist when and where desired, but could also unite or merge with others. Thus the cybercosm, the integrated system of machines, computers, robots, and sophotects, was a vast One with countless mutable avatars. Its apex became the Teramind, an intellect inconceivable to mortals and constantly growing.

The cybercosm did not enslave humanity—why should it?—nor did humans regard themselves as parasites on it. It had a single vote in the parliament of the World Federation, together with an advisory role. People had their own lives to lead. The cybercosm was simply their invaluable partner. To be sure, it was nothing but good sense to follow the counsel of the machine mind. In this wise had the world, uncoerced, become stable, peaceful, prosperous, and happy. Don't worry about scattered malcontents here and there. Don't wonder what the ultimate purposes of the Teramind may be; they are utterly abstract, remote from any concerns of flesh and blood. . . .

Not that the cybercosm was entirely separate from humanity. Besides all of its aspects that were in direct contact, it had its intermediaries, the synnoionts. Those were men and women of suitable innate capabilities, raised from childhood to be a part of it, repeatedly in electrophotonic rapport with it. They interpreted between the two kinds of intelligence. Often they became important officers of the Federation. But power in itself did not interest them. Their promised reward was that, if accident did not intervene, at the end of life they would be downloaded into the Oneness.

Then the world learned of the existence of Proserpina, an asteroid, but a huge one and of high density. Long since cast by Jupiter into an orbit that took nearly two million years to complete, it was now in the far reaches of the Solar System, among the comets of the Kuiper Belt and outward bound for the Oort Cloud. Even so, it offered habitation, with the resources of those comets to draw upon, to Lunarians, at such a distance from Earth that they could again have an independent nation. Many of them emigrated there.

So matters stood when Nicol was born. Or so, at any rate, he rendered them. He thought with a flash of sardonicism that he wasn't lying much when he called the whole account a fiction, as far short as it fell of the richness of reality.

After another silence, Borges shook his head. "No," he said, "I am sorry, but I can make nothing of this."

Nicol curbed the impulse to cry out that he had not spun a yarn nor tried to forecast. "Too fantastic?" he asked.

"Actually, no. As I listened, I harked back to the past. How surreal would this city, this room appear to a hunter in the Ice Age, or even to a Martín Fierro? In my work I have never been closely concerned with modern science and engineering, but I can conceive the possibilities are as grandiose as you describe. What would baffle me is the people who live with them and in them. They would inevitably be more foreign than any dweller in Karnak or Cambaluc."

"You've dealt with foreigners in your writing, sir."

"I took them out of myself. They were facets of me. What else can a writer do? If your future world did exist—and you have indeed at some moment sounded like a veritable time traveler"—Borges smiled—"then I should have to know its inhabitants far better before I could abstract imaginary characters from them, or even compose a lyric about them, and I have not enough life span left to make such an acquaintance."

They are too alien, Nicol thought. I am too alien.

"I can perhaps say that I would not envy a poet in their mainstream civilization," Borges murmured. "I think my advice would be that he seek elsewhere."

And then: "Well, we have had quite an unusual talk, and I thank you for it, but—"

Nicol glanced at his spring-powered armband watch. "Of course. I hope I haven't overstayed my welcome." His allotted real time was indeed getting short. And Borges would naturally have wanted to go home, have lunch and perhaps a siesta, and work with his translator.

The program would stop running.

"Not at all. A pleasure." As gracious as always, Borges made small talk for some additional minutes. At the end, almost shyly, he asked, "Would you like a little souvenir of this occasion?" With hands grown skilled in darkness, he took from a drawer a copy of *El libro de arena*, signed it, and gave it to his caller.

That was the most heartbreaking of everything. Nicol shook hands in a daze, mumbled farewell, and made his way back to the mirage street.

He had not walked far when it vanished, he fell through an instant of night, and again he lay in the tank.

Mechanically, lost from his surroundings, he let the attendant help him out and detach the connections. The bath fluid rolled straight off his skin into an absorber. He dressed, left, and went down the corridors, barely noticing where he was. Sometimes he glanced down at his hand, as if it held a book.

Why this feeling of nullity, of loss and grief? Surely not disappointment. He wasn't that childish, was he? It had been clear from the first how slight his chances were of learning anything useful to him. He had had an encounter with a ghost of greatness. That ought to be enough, and a fountainhead of new strength. Instead, his loneliness had redoubled.

Loneliness—no, isolation. Estrangement from his world and from his own spirit.

The foyer was empty, oppressively still. He didn't want the enclosure of his room, either. With a muttered curse, he went outside.

Night had long since fallen. A full Moon rode high in a cloudless heaven. It made the land a witchery of sable and argent. Across distances the mist lifted hoar from the falls. Air lay cool, pervaded by their thunder.

Once more an impulse swooped and seized. Nicol set forth, bound yonder.

Moonlight illuminated the trails and catwalks. Where trees whose crowns it frosted overshadowed them, the informant on his wrist produced a flashbeam for him, thin but sufficient if he went carefully. His muscles rejoiced to be moving. He followed the whole way to the overlook at the Garganta del Diablo. There he stood for a time out of time, looking, listening, being.

The wonder spread before him and around him, titanic

reach of cliffs down which the cataracts rushed and roared, agleam below the Moon, lesser streams hastening to meet them in the gorge, wildness, power, majesty, and at his back the forest full of murk and fragrances and over his head the stars.

Here was Earth, ancient Earth, mother of humankind and all other life, calling to the cosmos that begot her. The falls in their violence and splendor echoed the birth of suns and planets from shining nebulae, of the universe as it exploded from primordial nothingness and there was light.

A diamond point crossed the sky, low above the northern horizon, some orbiting satellite, and that also was right, it belonged. At the present phase of the Moon he could not see any gleam from cities on it, nor could he find Mars or Alpha Centauri, but that didn't matter, he knew that humans were there also. As for the machines, the omnipresent machines, robots, sophotects, Teramind, tonight he refused to fret. They were what they were, he was what he was.

Whatever that might be, he thought with a return of ruefulness.

Yet his heart was still high when he started back toward his bed. The grandeur had entered him, and he believed that the phantom had in truth counseled him well. Seek elsewhere. The variousness open to him was well-nigh unbounded. Someplace in it he might find what he needed.

Or he might fail. He recognized that that was more likely, and that then anger might prove his undoing. But first he would have tried, he would have sought.

CHAPTER

1

A dead man spoke with a machine.

Yes, I understand why the Oneness has raised me back into being. Trouble is loose, and again there is need for me to go to and fro in the world. But tell me what and how, that I may do my work as soon as may be and return to the Oneness.

Yet he was not truly dead, nor truly a man. Before he who sometimes called himself Venator perished, the cybercosm had downloaded the configurations of his mind into the program of a neural network that mapped his brain; and meanwhile it gave the aged flesh a sleeping away into cessation. For a span thereafter, the consciousness was an electrophotonic intelligence in an organo-metallic body. That was only a span, to accustom it to its new condition. Then, as had been promised the living man, he got his reward for faithful service. The cybercosm merged the mind with itself.

Identity regained was, at first, bitter and bewildering.

The reply ran: *Our great peace lies once more under threat. Someone or something has breached the walls of our inmost secrets.* Those were not material walls, Venator knew. They were encryptions and lines of communication that ought to have been secure against all that the laws of nature allowed to exist. A strange genius had found ways to corrupt the very system. *We know this from the fact that there has been more activity, not our own, than can be accounted for by quantum fluctuations; and that was determined only lately. Thus we do not know what files have been ransacked, or for what purpose, save that it cannot be benign.*

And the speaker was not truly a machine, a sophotect with individuality. It was a part or aspect of the central intelligence—not the actual Teramind, of course, but distantly joined to that apex through nodes of ascending power. So is the forefinger of a human a distinct thing while also a component of her hand, which is a component of her arm, which is a component of her entire organism. But this mind could, when desired, become one with as many others as necessary to deal with any question or any danger. What it was now was merely what it deemed to be sufficient.

And neither of these two was truly speaking. Directly linked, they exchanged information and thoughts at well-nigh the speed of light. In less than a second, Venator knew what had gone on in the thirty years since his death, saw what it might portend, and realized what he must do.

But let words stand in for that lightninglike discourse. It is not altogether a false analogy. As he settled into his re-created state, Venator began to remember how it had felt being human, how it had felt to talk.

—Almost surely this business is centered on the Moon, and most likely the virusmaster is there. Little active hostility to the order of things remains on Earth, and it is ideational or emotional—ill informed, ill organized where it is organized at all, devoid of any significant resources. But ever more Lunarians grow ever more restless. No longer simply expressing dissent, refusing cooperation with Terrans, or evading what laws of their republic they can, increasingly often they openly violate those laws that do not please them; and acts of sabotage are occurring. Although agents of the Peace Authority have not succeeded in discovering what the membership of the Scaine Croi is, they estimate it in the thousands, and certainly its sympathizers include most of the race.

—But the Lunarians are a dwindling minority, a dying breed. Or so they were toward the end of my life. What menace can they offer?

—Their birth rate is rising anew. They are getting back a belief in their future. It is the influence of Proserpina, direct and indirect, that inspires them. What else? This was foreseen and feared already in your day.

—Proserpina is so remote, though, so small and poor. The colony was a desperate gamble. We thought it might well fail. At worst, it should not have posed a serious problem for centuries to come. What has changed yonder?

—The colony has struck firm roots. Its population

prospers and slowly enlarges. Left to itself, it can reach equilibrium and survive indefinitely.

—We meant to see to it that that would be the probable outcome: an equilibrium, a tiny and static nation isolated in the far fringes of the Solar System, insignificant and virtually forgotten by the rest of humankind.

—Exactly. Thus far our policies have worked well. Proserpina is contained. Resentment among its people was expected and allowed for. What was not properly expected was the degree to which that resentment would infect the Lunarians on Luna.

—Hm. *I* could have guessed it. Proserpina may be invisible to them, but in spirit it blazes forth that their old wild ways are still alive, still free. Humans who rebel are not those without hope, but those who suppose that at last they see the end of the tunnel.

—You can well judge, who have been human yourself.

—Terran human. Lunarians are not like me. (Memory stirred, a Lunarian woman walked again with her red hair and wicked laughter, the download must set aside a download's equivalent of pain.) Nevertheless, I think that they and I are akin in this.

—They are not insane. There is no reason to anticipate insurrection on the Moon. However, the violation of our databases clearly indicates an organization both strong and cunning, with tendrils into the cybercosm. It also indicates enmity, not so? Both these point toward the Scaine Croi.

—What action has the Peace Authority taken?

—Intensive investigation. (Details followed, not a welter of them but a coherent, mathematically precise representation.) As you see, progress has been slight. The special capabilities of a download, halfway between the organic and the cybernetic, could prove of critical importance. Your record, your gifts and skills and experiences while alive, singled you out. Therefore you have been resurrected.

—Agents with Terran genes would certainly have . . . difficulty . . . penetrating a Lunarian underground. Also, that outfit will maintain its private lines of communication. Meanwhile, any Lunarian willing to dissemble a bit, or just key in to the public database, can learn about most of the things Terrans are doing. Yes-s-s.

—Another possible indication: Lirion is bound back for Luna.

—Lirion of Zamok Zhelezo? . . . No, wait, that was the family stronghold at Ptolemaeus. He went to Proserpina and founded Zamok Drakon. We met, he and I, a few times, on his first return to the inner System.

—This will be his third.

—After so many years? He stirred up ample trouble earlier, but we never got enough evidence to arrest him and he went freely home. I bade him good-bye. If cats could smile, he would have been smiling like a cat. Oh, no, he has not come back for nothing.

—The temptation is to seize him and brainphase his knowledge out of him, legality or no. But he doubtless has emergency means, such as blowing his skull to bits, and we have no idea what his disappearance might trigger.

—Besides, he in himself may provide a spoor to follow into the heart of whatever this conspiracy is. I will seek him out, and then we shall see.

Through Venator's ghost went the olden thrill of the hunt.

CHAPTER

2

—Earth overhead in a hollow halidom,
Bone-studded stone—
With a curse, Jesse Nicol bade the recorder in his helmet cancel. The lines he had been composing went out of existence. He wished he could annihilate them as easily in his memory.

His aim had not been to capture the scene in words. It was too familiar; and forever too awesome. He stood at Beynac Point on the northern rim of the Tycho ringwall, awaiting his beloved. Southward, rock sloped down toward the crater floor it shadowed; afar lifted the central peak, up into darkness and crowned with stars. They were gentle of contour, those heights, eroded by millennial cosmic infall, but mighty of mass. Northward the rampart fell in highlights and glooms to a land where meteorite splash lay like hoarfrost and mountains marked the horizon. There Earth shone aloft, three-quarters full, blue-and-white marbled glory, brilliance to wash all stars from her part of heaven.

His breath and heartbeat were a susurrus lost within a silence as vast as that sky. Yet everywhere works of humankind thrust into sight, radio masts agleam, monorails tracing bright streaks, domes and hemicylinders at the junctures of roads, microwave dishes hurling invisible energy from dayside to the mother world, things tiny at their distances, toylike, widely strewn, but everywhere. The Habitat passed slowly across upward vision. The solar sails that held it in its otherwise unstable orbit around the Moon outshone any sister planet.

As Nicol watched, it entered the shadow cone, dimmed, and disappeared. For an instant the vanishment of his childhood home stirred him to eagerness. The symbol he needed—?

His hope had been to make what was around him speak somehow to the spirit. The poem should evoke what was here and what was past, life born and dying and relentlessly born again in extinction after extinction through billionfold years, spilling forth into space and finding that to live it must make itself alien to itself; and thereby the poem should raise up the truth that the spirit is always a stranger and alone, with nothing to keep it alight but whatever bravery it can bring into reality—No, not so flat, not so shallowly obvious; he would weave a music to sing what cannot be said.

The idea flickered out, useless. "Damn," he mumbled in archaic Anglo, "damn, damn, and God damn." Rage tasted acid on his tongue.

After a minute or two he calmed down enough to bark a laugh. He knew full well how easily fury could seize him, and this was ridiculous. A moonflitter pilot frustrated because his verses wouldn't come right!

At least he knew better than to dwell on how he had suffered the same defeat over and over, for as long as he could remember. Let him instead look forward to Falaire's arrival. When she wasn't at the trailhead where they were to meet, he had keyed the bulletin screen there and learned that some last-minute business would detain her for about an hour. He had entered a message in reply, that he would hike on up to this lookout. It had seemed a chance to think, feel, work on that which was within him.

Now he thought the poem would never take shape. Oh, yes, he could salvage bits of imagery that weren't too bad and give them a framework competently built; but why? The thing would be dead, with nothing of the horror or the austere hopefulness he had intended. To hell with it—another archaism, very suitable, as anachronistic as his dreams. The way of a man with a maid did not go outmoded.

"Time," he ordered, aloud rather than by touch. His informant replied likewise: "1432." Falaire was half an hour later than she'd recorded she would be. Nicol sighed, then wryly grinned. She was no more predictable than most Lunarians. She might even be legitimately delayed.

He tried to contemplate the view for its own sake.

Earthlight poured over a tall young man, caucasoid Terran, thin to the point of gauntness although springily muscled. Gray eyes looked from a sallow hatchet face. He kept his beard inhibited and his black hair short. His voice when he spoke was a somewhat harsh tenor. Thus had his DNA made him, and he disdained to get any changes, whether cosmetic or basic.

Magnificent desolation, he thought. What a wonderful phrase. And not from a poet; from a perfectly straightforward Apollo astronaut, centuries and centuries ago, blurted forth when first he espied this realm. The time had been right, the achievement happening, the man in and of it; and so the words came, not after struggle and soul-search but as if by themselves. *O daughter of Zeus, howsoever you know of these matters, tell me.*

"Jesse, aou!"

The clear soprano, ringing in his sonors, made him whirl around. Up the trail toward him came Falaire. Her low-gravity lope seemed to him more as if she danced, or even flew. That was not really because the solar collectors and cooling surfaces outspread from the lifepack between her shoulders resembled dragonfly wings. Nor was it because the silvery space suit, mostly bionic, fitted the slim curves of her like a second skin. It was herself, gracefulness and impulsiveness embodied.

She drew to a halt before him. For a moment they looked at one another. She was a trifle on the short side for a Lunarian woman, topping him by just three centimeters, but the features within the transparent helmet were purely of her race, face high in the cheekbones and tapering to a narrow chin, short and slightly flared nose, full mouth, ears that were not convoluted like his, great oblique eyes changeably green beneath arching tawny brows. Hair that was deep blond under daylike light fell in ashen waves past snow-fair skin that here was tinged a faint blue. He felt himself in the presence of faerie.

"Uh, well beheld," he greeted at last. The lilting Lunarian words dropped awkwardly off his tongue. He had mastered the language enough for practical purposes, but knew how far beyond him the subtleties were. Sometimes he lapsed into Anglo or Spanyó because he couldn't find a native phrase and perhaps it didn't exist.

Well beheld indeed, he thought, and added in haste, lest he gape at her, "How went your doings?"

She spread her fingers. A Terran would have shrugged. "Down some roads unforeseen." She did not explain, nor apologize for making him wait. Instead, she laughed. "We were to fare around afoot. Come. So much talktime has brewed unrest in my blood."

She set off along the rim trail. He went beside her silent until he ventured, "It is as beautiful as they say."

She glanced at him. "You have indeed not betrodden it erenow? I thought everyone in Tychopolis had"—which meant at least a hundred thousand—"as well as visitors from elsewhere."

"I've only walked it once, in the opposite direction from Beynac Point and only as far as Starfell. Of course, I have followed the whole circuit on the vivifer."

"*Followed.*"

He heard the scorn, and bridled a bit. "I don't pretend that was the real thing." A full-sensory simulacrum was still merely a simulacrum. The illusion of an actual experience that a dreambox gave was still merely an illusion. "But how many chances have I had? How often have I been here, for how long at a time?"

She laughed again. "Beware. Those prickles could pierce your suit." Briefly, she took his arm. "I promised I'd show you a byway that's not in the common database." A shout: "Hai-ach!" And she was off at a full, bounding run.

Barely able to keep up, the breath harsh in his throat, he felt anew how clumsy he was, how ill fitted for this world of hers. His ancestors had not been changed in their genes so that they could keep their health and bear live children under the gravity, nor had they evolved through generations a way of living and thinking and feeling that was unitary with their stark land.

And yet nearly all the rather few people they passed on the trail were Terrans. Some had been born and spent their early years on Earth; for most it had been the high-weight zone of the Habitat. Permanently settled on the Moon, they required nanomaintainors to hold the cells and fluids of their bodies in balance, with stiff regular exercises to keep their bones and muscles from atrophying. Nevertheless the Moon was their home, they had made it over as they chose, and Lunarians long since outnumbered could do little more than resent them. A fresh pang of sympathy for the metamorphs struck into Nicol. He too was a man without a birthright.

He did see two or three besides the woman who soared ahead of him. One led a moonwolf on a leash. That was a rare sight. Only a Lunarian would want such a vacuum-adapted beast, and hardly any owned them these days—

too expensive, if nothing else. Nicol wondered what coursings this man took his pet on, across the hills and into the craters. Who was he? Surely of Selenarchic descent, like Falaire, but unlike her family, he must have retained a fragment of former wealth.

When she finally halted, nobody else was in view. She had veered onto a side path that switchbacked down the outer ringwall until it came to an end at a narrow ledge. Dust puffed up from the regolith under their boots, was repelled by their outfits, and settled. It did not fall fast, but there was no air to hinder it. Stone hulked into the sky behind. Ahead, it slanted down toward a wastescape where the sole token of humanity was a transmission tower, reduced by remoteness to a metallic spiderweb.

They'd stopped scarcely soon enough, Nicol admitted to himself, annoyed. His heart thudded, his gullet was dry fire, his knees were about to give way. *She* just drew long breaths. A slight sheen of perspiration on her face caught the Earthlight, and somehow her locks had become tousled. He remembered her in bed, and vexation went from him. She was what she was. Let him bless fortune that for some reason she liked him.

He would not, dared not admit weakness. "In truth a . . . a ramble," he managed to croak.

She smiled. "Gallantly spoken. Shall we take refreshment? I brought wine."

He wanted very much to sit down, but she did not. "Water first," he commanded. The unit rose to his lips and he drank and drank. The chill revived him as much as did the wetness. She uncoiled a pair of tubes on a bottle at her hip and plugged them into their helmet locks. He thought how her fingers had once stroked across his lips.

The wine was noble, full-bodied, perhaps akin to a sauvignon blanc. He needn't be ashamed to say, "I don't recognize this. Where has it been hiding from me?"

She smiled straight into his gaze. "No synthetic. From the Yanique vineyard beneath Copernicus, held by the phyle that founded it. The lord of Acquai does not sell what they make, he bestows it on whom he will."

None of whom were Terrans, Nicol guessed. "You honor me."

"Nay. It's friendship." She slipped to his side and laid an arm around his waist. He did likewise. Sensors in the suit made it almost like holding her directly.

Almost. "That's the trouble with being topside," he said, "this stuff between us," and noticed that his jape had been in Anglo.

She understood and laughed, although she replied in her own tongue. "Eyach, save the eagerness for when we have the right environs."

His sudden happiness began to ebb. "That is too seldom," he mumbled, returning to Lunarian.

She nodded. "Yes, I am a-busied more than I might wish."

He wondered. Her work? Like him, she was in the Rayenn—and of it, as no Terran would ever be. She served as a liaison with outsiders of both species, the sort of public relations, intelligence gathering, and counseling that no sophotect could quite have handled. However, she appeared to operate mostly on her own, dealing with people and taking time off pretty well as she pleased. Lunarians were typically more interested in results than in procedures.

(Appeared? No, surely that was what she did. He could not imagine her condescending to take employment on any other terms. After all, her folks were of the Selenarchs, who had dominated the Moon when it was a sovereign nation. Her father still clung to a scrap of the estate at Zamok Orel in Lacus Somniorum. Nicol could imagine how grimly the old man struggled to maintain a castle gone empty, on nothing but his citizen's credit, and how poisonously it must gall him to accept that from the government. He had heard that her brother had given up and was spending his own entitlement income on pleasuring himself to death in Tsukimachi. Falaire might have done the same, or might have lived a life more prudent and equally meaningless. She chose to win something better for herself than modest comfort, for she possessed the drive and the capabilities to get real work and succeed in it. But no, she would never let any boss monitor her hours. Leave that to Terrans.)

Her words jarred him out of his thoughts. "You, though? What, no other woman?" Was that a gibe? "You're not a-space for any lengthy whiles."

"No," he snapped. As if by mutual consent, they let go and stepped apart. He shouldn't have replied so churlishly. The implied question had touched a nerve and he didn't want to answer it. His women had in fact been few, because few had especially interested him, any more than most men did. She was different. Therefore she could hurt him. Since meeting her he had not even patronized a joyeuse. He sought to change the subject. "Who is?"

In his mind, the robots and sophotects that took ships between the planets didn't count. How many of those were left, anyway? Spaceflight was dying out, being phased out, no longer much needed or wanted. Someday, he supposed, it would be one with the building of pyramids or the grazing of cattle. On Mars and Luna, too, machines had taken over transportation. Only the Rayenn was left in human hands, and that was only a courai.

(Flittingly he considered the word, for it had never gotten entirely within his comprehension, no matter that it now occupied his days. The organization was not really a company or a guild engaged in conveyance. It was an alliance of Lunarian magnates, with their underlings, as much for security and influence as for a profit that was marginal at best. Lunarian shippers and travelers used it more for the sake of pride and clannishness than because it was genuinely competitive with the cybernetic lines. The ceremonies and traditions it maintained, some of which went back to Fireball Enterprises, were for none but Lunarians. . . . It was sheer luck that the Rayenn needed a few Terrans and he had the innate ability to acquire the necessary skills. Generally his flights were hops, suborbital between points on the surface or up to the Habitat and back. But every now and then a job demanded higher accelerations than Lunarians could readily tolerate. . . .)

Once again her voice recalled him. Damnation, he thought, why this foul humor, why this wandering off on paths he had already trampled into ruts, when here he stood with Falaire? "They often are at Proserpina," she was saying.

Her face had turned eastward, away from Earth's brilliance. Did he see rapture? Stars gleamed yonder. "Yes," he replied slowly, "they make long voyages. They have to."

"And they wish!" she exclaimed. "It is their desire."

Their need, he refrained from insisting. The comets that they mined for ice, organics, and minerals were plentiful but spread through the immensities of Kuiper Belt and Oort Cloud. Not that the settlers on the iron asteroid minded traversing such reaches, he supposed. They or their parents had chosen to go dwell in eternal night. If they had not automated their spacecraft, that too must be a choice of theirs, perhaps because they feared creating another cybercosm. Still, Nicol wondered how souls so fierce and mercurial passed the time aboard.

"They don't often wish to come back to Luna," he remarked, largely to keep silence at bay. "When did their last ship before this new arrival call, seven years ago? Of course, that's a minimum four and a half months in transit," if the vessel went under boost the whole distance, extravagantly, at a full Lunar gravity. "Oh, no longer than an average comet mission, I should imagine—"

She swung upon him. He saw the quick ire he had come to know too well. "The energy cost, you clotbrain! They're forced to be niggard with fuel, reserve it for work that is vital—"

"I know—"

"—or for simple survival. And now this embargo laid on them!" Her rage spat at the lovely blue planet above. "Earth, Earth's machine overlord, would fain strangle them!"

"No, no, not that," he demurred, "not truly." He curbed a reminder to her that Proserpina had its fusion power plants, robotic factories, chemical and biological industry, nanotechnics, everything required to keep life alive. What claim had the inhabitants on a continued supply of antimatter? If Earth was terminating production, that was because Earth, Luna, and Mars had reached an equilibrium economy and no longer needed so concentrated an energy source, while the Proserpinans had nothing to trade for it. If they must therefore cease expanding, strike a balance between their own population and resources, settle down forever on their single miniature world, why, that would be evolution, natural selection at work.

Yet extinction had claimed some splendid creatures, mammoth, saber-tooth, great-antlered Irish elk; and it seemed to Nicol that eagles or tigers, existing on narrow ranges under strict protection, were not what their natures meant them to be. He would not argue with Falaire's anger.

Her tone quieted. "Eyach, I am a Lunarian," she sighed. "I was born aggrieved." As swiftly as it had flared, her temper cooled. A chuckle rang forth. "We came not topside for that, you and I, did we? Come, here is where we leave the trail."

He welcomed a release of tension. Glancing at the descent, he did have to say, "It looks tricky."

"It is," she answered merrily. "Ho-ay!" She sprang.

He swallowed his misgivings and followed, as cautiously as was consistent with not appearing timid. This section of the ringwall sloped steeply. Millennial small meteorite impacts had roughened it barely enough to provide footing. Under Earth weight he would soon have fallen, and even here a person could slip, roll, and plunge off a break to his death. The dust that, most places, held tracks for thousands of years, existed only in separate spatters. Yet Falaire leaped from point to precarious point with antelope sureness and speed.

Having reached her destination, a worn-down crag like thousands of others, she waited till he arrived panting and shaky. "Take ease," she invited.

"I didn't expect . . . you'd act this way . . . topside also," he got out.

She raised her brows. "Also?" she asked, half-archly.

"I'm told that you fly in the Devil Sky."—not a park where folk secured wings to themselves and flapped calmly aloft, but a cave where random violent winds were generated and a common sport was to try knocking somebody else a-spin. Every year saw numerous injuries and several fatalities.

For an instant, rancor spoke again. "What else have I to do for amusement, in this my cage?"

She had a certain bleak justice on her side, he thought. The genes that made her a Lunarian, to whom Luna was natural, had given her a Lunarian psyche as well. Nicol was not the first Terran to think that it was almost as if her kind were descended not from apes but from cats, or perhaps wolves. When the modern world thrust upon them such modern things as democracy or the prohibition of private revenge, it had been like a trainer in an ancient circus making a leopard learn tricks. Generations of the animals had doubtless lived thus, more safely and prosperously than in the wild, but within them smoldered al-

ways the leopard heart. Lunarians, being human, knew
what their condition was.

Well, you could not let carnivores prowl your streets
after dark, could you?

Falaire finger-shrugged. "No matter today," she said.
"I've brought you to what I promised to show you. First I
bind you anew to hold the secret of it, as you swore erstwhile. We'd not have tourists enter, whether by vivifer or
in yawping, gawping person."

He wondered what landmarks she had used to find it,
and how the knowledge of it had stayed hidden this long.
With a slight chill, he felt the alienness of her, whose love-
making had burst over him like none he ever knew among
his own kind. "You, you honor me, my lady," he stammered.

Did warmth touch her words? "I've come to think you
trustworthy." It was the highest compliment she had yet
paid him. Mostly she had simply remarked that she enjoyed his company and his body—when she was in the
mood for them. He had not risked saying anything that
went deeper.

She took his hand and led him on, carefully now. The
crag and an overhang behind it masked a crevice. They
squeezed through and turned on their lamps. He gasped.
Around him lay space enclosed by crystals, as if he stood
in the cavity at the middle of a huge geode. They glit-
tered, sparked, refracted light into a million shifting bits
of rainbow. When he touched them their edges and
points were knife-keen. He imagined he felt the electric
thrill that the photons awakened, making their atoms
sing.

"Why, this is a miracle," he whispered.

"Say rather, a charming whim of the universe." Her mirth mocked his awe.

"The geologists—how would they explain it?"

"They shall have no call to."

Those who thus hoarded scientific treasure were indeed alienated, he thought, and shuddered a little.

Then he lost himself in the marvel. Two hours had passed when they left it and climbed back to the rim trail.

Falaire glanced aloft. He knew she could tell time by the terminator on Earth and by what stars the planet left visible. "We must turn home," she said.

Cheer had welled up in him, down among the jewels. "I've no objection," he laughed.

"I'll be occupied elsewhere this evenwatch," she replied without expressing regret.

Dashed, he gulped before he asked, "Would that be with Lirion?"

He hoped so, oh, he hoped so. In the ten daycycles since he arrived, the captain from Proserpina had been closeted with one Lunarian after another, some prominent, some obscure. They included leaders of the Rayenn. It would be logical to consult Falaire, who moved in her work between the Lunarian and the Terran worlds. Maybe it was Lirion she had seen just before she joined Nicol today.

"Nay," he heard, "with Seyant."

The news took him by the throat. In spite of common sense and all his resolutions, he cried, "What have you to do with *him?*"

That smug rotworm, he wanted to snarl. I'd kill him if I could. I'd drop him from orbit and watch him splash.

★   ★   ★

They met through her. She and Nicol had been wandering down a path in the wilderness below this crater. It was soon after they got acquainted, that wondrous chance meeting in the Rayenn's local ground control station. Already something glowed between them.

The cavern would have reached beyond sight, had they been able to look straight across its floor. Trees walled them in, Lunar-gravity high, elm and oak and white birch, broken by occasional canebrakes and small flower-studded meadows. Leaves rustled overhead, parted their vaults to give a glimpse of sky as blue and sun as bright as if they had been real, drew back together in the breeze and cast shadows speckled with light. A squirrel ran fiery up a trunk, a butterfly went past like a tiny flag, a daybat winged in pursuit of a glitterbug. Soil lay soft underfoot, breathing fragrances forth into coolness. She walked hand in hand with him as Ianeke had done on Earth.

They rounded a bend and there Seyant came, toweringly tall, flaxen-haired, flamboyant of garb and feline of gait. Falaire hailed him. All three stopped in mid-path. He and she talked animatedly in a dialect Nicol could not follow. At length she made an introduction. Seyant stared down and murmured in flawless Anglo, as if the Terran would not understand any native speech, "Ah, yes, the Earthbaby you've mentioned." To him: "I'm told you are an acceptably competent transporteer."

Since then Nicol had gathered in his turn little more than that Seyant had independent means, over and above citizen's credit. Falaire sometimes quoted his witticisms. Whenever he met Nicol, he sank their barbs into the other man.

* * *

She replied sharply, "That which I mean to do."

With a wrenching effort, he curbed a rage he knew was unreasonable. "I'm . . . sorry," he muttered, but could not help adding, "I know I have no claim on you."

She nodded. "We are sundered by more than race, Jesse."

They started off on the path. "You could become more nearly one with us if you chose," she said after a while.

"With whom?" he rasped. "The Scaine Croi?" This was not the first hint she had dropped.

She regarded him, unwontedly grave. "You speak as if it were criminal to desire freedom."

She would despise him if he shammed. He would despise himself. "Freedom from what?"—when the Habitat bred Terrans who were glad of the World Federation.

"From the system," she said, "the cybercosm that, below all the mincing pretenses, rules over us."

"What would you have me do?" Sardonicism stirred. "Whatever it is, I'll probably have to say gracias, no. I own to a taste for melodrama, but only in the arts."

In real life, he knew—he had learned from trouble and grief—it was too strong a temptation.

"Maychance I will speak further, some other day-cycle," she said.

"Do, if you wish. Yes . . . please do." His caution broke apart. "I'm always happy to speak with you, Falaire."

Her smile went over him like the Earthlight. "Ay-ah, we shall that. Tomorrow evenwatch? And then again after your next flight, oh, I will find hours for you."

But *this* nightwatch—

"Meanwhile, you've other friends, nay?" she went on amiably. "They could receive you in that rowdy Uranium Dragon you showed me."

"Maybe," he grunted in Anglo.

"Or the Black Sword?"

"No!"

Alcohol was dangerous enough for him in his present temper. A den offering a drug more potent, such as exoridine, releasing all inhibitions, might cause him to attack somebody. Best might be if he stayed in his little apartment and got quietly drunk alone. Maybe, just maybe, a few verses would come to him that were not altogether worthless.

Once more Falaire tucked her arm under his. It was a foreign gesture to her, a Terran gesture, and so the more moving. "We've yet a span to go, you and I," she said. "Enjoy the sights."

His helpless wrath faded a bit. He could try. At least he had the sight of her, there beside him, profiled against stars.

He decided that later, whatever she wanted, he would let her tell him what she thought he could do for her cause, whatever it was. No harm in listening.

C H A P T E R

Hydra Square had changed little over the centuries, not at all in the forty years since Venator last crossed it. Then he had been alive, now he was a set of ongoing electro-photonic processes in a neural network that received its information through the sensors of the machine it walked in. But when he allowed for different perceptions, he experienced the same as before. Fish still swam colorful and algae still waved sinuous under the clear paving. The fountain at the center still spouted its whiteness at the simulated sky, water descending in sonic-pulsed serpen-tine curves and its own music. The doorways on three sides still led to museums, which scarcely anyone visited now. The municipal service establishments on the fourth side did not see much more use. The plaza was a relic, embalmed in time, because the life of Tychopolis had moved elsewhere.

·He found it overflowing not far down in·Tsiolkovsky Prospect. There too something of the old remained, duramoss underfoot, hard-surfaced lanes for motorskaters, three-level arcades of delicate pillars and arches— nothing more. The glowpanel ceiling no longer displayed shifting fantastical illusions, only chromatic abstractions culturally neutral. Most shops had been converted to tenements, crammed and raucous, although enterprises here and there displayed light-signs, animations, banners in their various alphabets, KAWAMOTO GYMNA- SIUM, BENGALI HOUSE RESTAURANT, TANJAY CASINO, LI YUAN TONG, WEIN UND WEIBER, HARMONIC COUNSELING, PYONGYANG VO- LUPTUARY, SONGGRAM & CO., ISKUSSTVO I TAIINA, or things that even he did not recognize. His chemosensors told him that the very odors had changed, no longer subtle perfumes and smokes but simply of human bodies; nor did melodies drift eerily through the air.

Hardly a Lunarian was in the throngs that hurried, jostled, gesticulated, chattered, dickered, laughed, sorrowed, kept silence, busy or idle or lost in some narcotic dream. They were as diversified as Earth itself, a dark man in a turban beside a dark woman in a sari, a portly brown person in sarong and blouse, a blond in form- fitting iridescence, a woman concealed by gown and veil, a man with a pearl-button cap above an embroidered robe, another who wore feathers and bird mask, a body-painted nude, motley and bells on one who capered, a woman bearing clan emblems on her breasts and a claymore across her back, on and multitudinously on. Unisuits, tunics, or other ordinary garb were commonest, but not by much. During his life Venator had watched people differentiate into ever more societies, some occupying their own regions, some no less distinct for being global. It started before he was born and continued further after he died. He thought that humans were driven to make whatever uniqueness, belongingness, communal and individual identity they could within the leveling huge impersonality of World Federation and cybercosm.

And yet they weren't unhappy, he thought. Who in their right minds would want a return of war, poverty, rampant criminality, disease, famine, cancerously swelling population, necessity to work no matter how nasty or deadening the work might be, mass lunacy, private misery, and death in less than a hundred years? It was the metamorphs and their few full-human adherents who were the malcontents, the troublemakers—Lunarians above all, but others too, perhaps more dangerous because less obvious. . . .

No one hailed him as he proceeded, everyone made way, not in fear or humility but a natural, courteous deference. The body he employed was an ordinary general-purpose model, two meters high where the sensory turret rose upon a smoothly curved chassis with four legs and four arms. It sheened a modest deep blue, trimmed in silver. Plain to see, though, it either housed or was under the remote control of an intelligence, whose linkages ultimately traced to the Teramind.

At a dropway he went down three levels to Lousma Passage. A short distance beyond was the hotel he sought, where flickerlight characters spelled SHIH TIEN GAN above an ornate door. The lobby scanned him, found in its database that he was expected, gave him Captain Lirion's suite number, and admitted him to the appropriate corridor. When he reached the door there it immediately retracted, closing again behind him.

The chamber he entered was furnished in Lunarian style and luxuriously spacious. Someone had transferred a substantial amount of credit, he thought. The man from Proserpina stood awaiting him. "Well beheld," Lirion greeted.

His tone was, if not cordial—a mannerism his race seldom displayed anyway—at least interested, and he smiled for a moment. "My thanks, *donrai*," Venator replied in the same language. He chose the honorific carefully, to imply equivalent if not identical status. He could have spoken idiomatic Lunarian, but kept his range of expressions limited. Why demonstrate more abilities than he must?

"I cannot offer you refreshment, can I?" Lirion murmured. A gibe?

Venator formed a chuckle. "Hardly. But refresh yourself if you like."

"I do and will." Lirion went to a spidery table on which stood a carafe and goblets.

As he poured and sipped, Venator studied him. He was of characteristic Lunarian male stature, two meters, long-limbed, well formed, erect in diamond-dusted black tunic and hose. Pale brown features showed more Asian ancestry in their bones than was usual, but the big oblique eyes were amber-hued and the hair that fell to his shoulders was grizzled bronze. Otherwise, only a leanness in face and hands betokened an age approaching the century mark.

"I hope you are comfortable and content here," Venator said. The banality was another move to disarm wariness. Likewise had he come in person, rather than call on the eidophone or summon this visitor to Authority headquarters.

"It has its differences from home. After many years agone, they strike at me," Lirion admitted. "But I am cosseted, and no longer cramped inside a spacecraft."

Alone, Venator remembered. Several months alone, accelerating and decelerating at one Lunar gravity. So immense was the distance. Light itself took three days. Well, most Lunarians minded solitude less than most Terrans did, and of course Lirion would have had a database full of books, music, shows, games, perhaps pastimes more esoteric, quite possibly a dreambox. The ship ran herself; companions for him would have meant more mass to boost, more precious antimatter to spend.

But then why was the ship so large? There must be carrying capacity for several people, including life support, and for tonnes of cargo. When asked upon arrival, Lirion said casually that this had been what was available. Venator doubted that. He badly wanted an excuse to go aboard and inspect.

"Yes, it has ever been good to come back," Lirion finished.

Each time to brew trouble, Venator thought.

Across his awareness flashed what biography his service had been able to piece together. Descended from the great Selenarchic rebels Rinndalir and Niolente, Lirion was born in Zamok Zhelezo at Ptolemaeus Crater. His father, who retained a certain amount of wealth, power, and connections, went into politics, struggling and conniving to keep the Moon from conversion into a republic in fact as well as in name. The establishment of the Habitat doomed that endeavor. Meanwhile, the existence of Proserpina had been revealed and the migration of disaffected Lunarians began. After his father's death in a brawl with Terran newcomers, Lirion took over management of the phratry's interests, which included a share in the Rayenn transport association. He was often in contact with Earthfolk. They liked him, deeming him a moderate. In reality, it now seemed, he was among the secret founders and leaders of the Scaine Croi. At age fifty he sold out his rapidly depreciating holdings and moved to Proserpina—among the last who did, as scant as was the antimatter left in Lunarian possession. He prospered yonder, building Zamok Drakon and founding a family that grew prominent in a revived Selenarchy. His gifts for organization and intrigue served him well, bringing him to the forefront of enterprises among the comets and in councils at home. Despite the abyss between, he maintained encrypted contact with unidentified persons on Luna; and sometimes he returned. . . .

"You should grace us oftener," Venator said.

"Belike it will not happen again," Lirion replied. "Passage in a ship with naught better than fusion to drive it would eat a twain of years or worse. I have not many left me."

And yet the Proserpinans had laid out what was necessary for this journey of his, Venator thought. "Your business is important, then."

"So thinks your service," Lirion answered dryly.

"The Peace Authority has a natural concern, yes."

"My mission was announced beforehand. I am here on behalf of my world to seek persuasion, that Earth provide us with more antimatter."

Not just for spacecraft motors, Venator knew. For heavy engineering works of every kind, to make Proserpina over. The iron core that gave it a gravity comparable to Luna's and offered riches to industry also made it monstrously more difficult to hollow out habitations than on this basaltic globe. "Pardon me if I ask elementary questions. Communications are thin, and your people have not been exactly forthcoming, you know. How small has your supply"—that the original settlers brought along—"gotten?"

"The end of it is in sight," Lirion said, which Venator judged rather noncommittal. "We have no access to Mercury, that we might forge our own."

A vision of the inmost planet rose before Venator. He had never been there. No living creature had, nor any machine that was not armored and specialized against its inferno. But the vivifer had presented it to him, had let his mind range the pocked and scarred terrain, through freezing nights and furnace days. From the nearby sun raged energy measurable but unimaginable, captured and brought to focus by huge installations across the land and up in orbit, an achievement worthy of gods. Photons slammed into nucleons, quantum convulsions went through the vacuum, newborn particles positive and negative hurtled down magnetic lines of force to their separate destinations—Operated at full capacity, the Mercurian plant had yielded hundreds of kilos of antimatter per Terrestrial day.

He no longer felt awed. Now he was a machine, and all machines were his kin. Although his reborn individual self did not comprehend, nor remember as more than fragments, what it knew when it was one with the cybercosm, he recalled how it had embraced the whole universe.

Yet that self was human too, with a feel for human things. He decided that enough polite phrases had passed back and forth, few though they were. If he piqued Lirion, he might provoke a reaction that would give him a little insight, a bit of a clue to the man's real intentions.

"Do you feel we owe you access?" he began, keeping his tone mild. "Your folk chose to go live on the fringe of deep space because they wanted no part of our civilization."

"We lack the means to follow Anson Guthrie to Alpha Centauri, like Rinndalir and his camarilla," Lirion responded as quietly. "Proserpina is the last hope of our breed in the Solar System, not to be engulfed and in the end go extinct."

Lunarians generally preferred challenge to blandness. "Have you then concluded that altruism is, after all, a virtue? You want this World Federation that you loathe to supply you, when you have nothing to exchange that we need."

"We wish for a single large consignment. Given that, the engineers say they can build a fusion-powered factory to make more, not as copiously as on Mercury, but sufficient."

"I ask you again, why should we? You're not dying of hunger or cold."

One rarely got a glimpse of a Lunarian's heart, if that was what Venator saw. "Better so, maychance, than what must happen if you deny us," Lirion told him somberly. "We foresee imprisonment, where we and all who stem from us are locked into eternal sameness, as adventurous and alive as barnacles on a stone."

"Have you no inner resources?"

"A machine spoke there," Lirion scoffed. "Abstractions, mental constructs, the Teramind admiring its own exaltedness, is that for living creatures? Behold Earth's gain for aiding us—a society new and strange, doing deeds and dreaming dreams to shake you out of your stagnation."

Yes, thought Venator, that is exactly what we fear. Aloud: "We think of it as equilibrium. World-weariness? Why, the world is so rich that no human lifetime is enough to explore all of it."

"You are satisfied, then—stabilized, you say. Lest new discovery threaten your order of things, you are ending antimatter production."

"Read in what motives you will. The plain fact is that it's no longer needed. We are caching a supply for any foreseeable contingencies." Venator paused. "The cache is thoroughly guarded, you understand. May I speak frankly? Power like that, in—uncontrolled—hands, is too risky, however distant from us they may be."

Lirion showed no umbrage. He laughed, a low trill in

his throat. "Eyach, you did not come here for us to toss clichés at one another."

"No. I hope to sound you out."

Lirion raised his brows. "In what wise?" He sipped his wine, savoringly, while he listened.

"You've announced your aim of persuading the Federation to release a quantity of antimatter to Proserpina. You're free to argue for that, of course. I daresay you have inducements to offer influential Terrans." Saying "bribes" would be impolite, and would doubtless amuse the Lunarian. "But you have been observed doing very little persuading, either on public channels or in private talks."

Lirion finger-shrugged. "I soon saw there was small point in it. Yes, Federation citizens may publish their words, elect their parliamentarians, debate in their committees, vote on their measures, but you know still better than I, it is the cybercosm that decides."

"Do you honestly think of it as our overlord? I can't believe that. You're intelligent and educated. You realize humans and machines are parts of the same system, and sophotects are individuals as conscious as you are."

"Nay, not quite thus. Their minds are avatars of the One, and it has come to have its own ends, which are not remotely human."

How could they be? thought Venator. "Is a hammer your enemy because it can drive a nail better than your fist? It's all mind evolving, human and machine together."

"Maychance, once humans have ceased to be human." Lirion made a chopping gesture. His voice, though, turned gentle, and he smiled. "Let us not stumble into philosophical dispute, alike tedious and bootless. Truth to say,"—if it was truth, Venator thought—"your coming raises a wisp of optimism. Can it be that through you the cybercosm will speak directly to me?"

A milligram of candor would be wise. "I'll be happy to convey any messages, but I am not a sophotect myself."

Lirion cocked his head. "So, a download? I suspected as much. Then I should in courtesy ask your name."

Venator would not explain that it wasn't that simple, that even in life he had been a synnoiont who from time to time entered into a communion with the cybercosm as full as was possible for an organic being. But he might as well be frank about things that meant nothing to the other. "Once I was Lucas Mthembu."

Unexpected memories came astir, a little cradle song of his mother's, a lion walking golden on a summer-golden veldt, the Brain Garden where he lost his childhood and gained his life's meaning, savory food and drink, stalking a killer down a nighted alley, fishing on a lake that sheened beyond the horizon, conflict, comradeship, Lilisaire of the flame-red mane, who tricked him to his sharpest defeat and lived on in him ever afterward—"But I've used many different tags since then. Venator will do."

No need to explain that it meant "hunter" in a language forgotten by all but the great database. Nor should Lirion know that this was not a straightforward download from a living human with which he dealt, but one copied back from its union with the One—Oh, longing for Nirvana!

"I would be most interested to hear whatever you care

to tell me about your life, Donrai Venator," the Lunarian
said. "And belike it would give me some helpful insights.
We are indeed isolated on Proserpina, out among comets
and stars."

Venator formed a laugh. "I shan't recite you an autobi-
ography. But yes, let's talk, let's get acquainted."

The conversation went on for two or three hours, lively
and pleasant in a sword's-point fashion. Each had much
to ask and much to relate. The Lunarian was by turns
discursive, incisive, pragmatic, lyrical, witty, always
charming. Venator recollected stories told of him while
he lived here, tales of a champion athlete and gō player,
ruthless entrepreneur and historical scholar, gourmet and
gourmand, sexually voracious and given to long spans
alone, corrupt politician, neo-feudal lord, dangerous con-
spirator, and, just possibly, idealist on behalf of his people. Although he was too haughty to boast, it grew clear
that after he moved to Proserpina his saga became an
epic.

Yet at the end almost nothing germane to the issue had
been said by either party. (*Almost* nothing.) There was a
desultory discussion of trade. (Would they not like more
water on Mars?—No, not at present, and should the need
arise, robots could go bring in a comet.) There was men-
tion of safeguards. (Surely any notion of warheads
launched from Proserpina against Earth, or vice versa,
was ridiculous!—Yes, but if ever violence broke out in
yonder deeps, an Earth that had supplied the means must
answer heavily to herself.) Both recognized the futility
and dropped the subjects. Lirion said he had talks scheduled with two more persons, but unless the government

relented, he expected soon to start home. Meanwhile, what Donrai Venator had remarked, concerning the status and encouragement of private ventures in a postcapitalist economy, was fascinating, and would he explain further? . . .

They parted company with expressions of mutual respect and goodwill. In life Venator had been able to make his face a fluid mask when he chose; but he was rather glad that now he had no face. As he walked back to headquarters, his mind went in full cry on the spoor of his quarry.

Already earlier he had winded scents. The intelligence corps of the Peace Authority numbered few Lunarians, none of whom would have been trusted in this business. No Terran could have trailed Lirion unnoticed, especially down into an old section where only Lunarians and other metamorphs lived. But maintainor robots went everywhere, as vital as breath and scarcely more heeded. Before Lirion landed, Venator had put observation programs into certain of them.

The man from Proserpina repeatedly, quietly made his way to an apartment in the old quarter. Sometimes he spent hours there. The place was leased to one Seyant, a Lunarian about whom little could be discovered except that he traveled a good deal, everywhere around the Moon.

It took considerable detective work on Venator's part—he was a bit surprised when he finally succeeded—but he learned that, about a year ago, equipment had been brought into the apartment and work had been done that indicated something to do with communications.

Since then, unbreakable quantum encryptions had often gone in and out. That was no crime, of course, nor very unusual, and Venator had no proof that anyone inside had been tapping into the government's secret database. It wasn't supposed to be possible.

However, once alerted, the system was able to sketch out several different ways in which it might be done. All required certain unique capabilities. Venator judged that, if his corps raided the apartment, they would not find a program for the purpose, or any other hard evidence. The information, whatever it was, *had* been stolen, the coded news had reached Proserpina, and Lirion was here to take charge of the operation—whatever it was.

What instructions had he sent in advance? Probably laser beams had been making their days-long journeys back and forth for years, tenuous threads slowly woven into a plot. Venator had no idea what the intent was; or else he had too many conflicting ideas. But the time for action must be drawing nigh, because Lirion said he would soon depart.

The corps might arrest him on grounds of suspicion, which might barely be tenable under the law, less in hopes of wringing out the truth—he must have provisions against that, a suicide bomblet merely the most obvious—than to upset the conspiracy. Venator was dubious whether that would work either. At best, it would leave the organization unprobed, intact, ready to wreak new mischief.

Today he had met with the ringleader. His human intuition, which no pure sophotect could quite have matched, confirmed him in a decision he had been nurturing. Surveillance was the method, secretly watching and listening to the enemy in his councils. It was his fortune to have a means available.

Ancient though the apartment was, its plans remained in the city's archival database, together with records of structural changes made over the centuries. Those were few. Terrans seldom cared to take over places meant for Lunarians, taller than they and with curious tastes in layout and decor. During a former period of unrest, tenants had installed heavy screening against all kinds of eavesdropping, which had subsequently been kept up-to-date. Later, others added what they presumably meant for an emergency bolt-hole. From a cabinet, a trap gave on a vertical shaft that led to a tunnel on the next level down, and so away through a labyrinth of fixed machines: air and water recyclers, pumps, thermal equalizers, and the like.

A sophotect in a miniature body had crept up into the cabinet and found that it was outfitted with camouflaged, passive optical and sonic fibers; a person there could look out into the main room and hear what went on. Venator felt sure the door was also concealed, indistinguishable from its wall. He had no reason to believe that anyone had used the facility for lifetimes, if ever. The spy reported finding no locks, detectors, alarms, or other precautions.

Perhaps the current occupants didn't know it existed, perhaps they had failed to give it thought. They were mortal, therefore fallible.

He would have himself smuggled in.

Not as he was. This body, or any that would hold his braincase, was too big, too metallic, much too noticeable electronically. A connection to the outside would also be. A quick foray for spying purposes was one thing, a prolonged stay was something else.

Once brought there, he must lurk alone, physically helpless, a box with nothing but speaker, sensors, and spirit. He dared not even post watchers in the neighborhood. An ultrasmall robot should be able safely to creep up to him about once per daycycle. If action seemed imminent, he would give it the sign to go fetch a larger one to remove him.

Otherwise, it could become a long while alone in the dark, but he had machine patience. Moreover, he had what no machine did, the subtle understanding, the ability to guess rightly what a word or a gesture implied, that came from memories of having been human.

As for the hazard—in his present state he was incapable of fear. What he did feel was glee. Until he gained his reward, the return to transcendent Oneness, next best was matching wits with an opponent such as Lirion.

CHAPTER

4

Jesse Nicol was haunted by his last evening in Oceania. He had been standing at the starboard rail of the upper promenade deck on the *Okuma 'Olo*, glaring west. It was less a ship than a town afloat, home to some four thousand people. Beneath him tiers went like a landscape, flower gardens aglow between hedges of close-trimmed privet or carefree lavender, bougainvillea and fuchsia brightening the white sides of cabins, rustly bamboo around the turf of hidden nooks, here and there a palm tree silhouetted against heaven, a stream splashing in small cataracts down to a pool where children frolicked. Their cries reached him, faint and sweet, as did the notes of a flute somewhere else, through air where a ghost of fragrance lingered while it cooled away toward nightfall.

Three similar communities lay in sight, widely spaced across the sea, and Nauru hove darkly on the northern horizon. Lights had begun to twinkle forth over the island. The Lahui Kuikawa had long since become too many for it, but it remained the heart of their nation. Near it the water was blanketed by aquaculture that stretched beyond sight. Elsewhere, waves ran low and whisperful, violet-blue with fragile foam streaks, molten-bright out where the sun came down to meet them.

A band of Keiki Moana swam by, pinniped incarnations of grace. Light from the west swirled in their wakes.

Nicol ignored them. He had ended an hour of solitary pacing to stop where he was and curse his destiny.

A soft footfall broke through to him. He turned about as Ianeke approached. For a moment they were still, he struggling to get rid of his thoughts, she uncertain.

"You stand lonely, Jesse," she said in Anglo. Her fluency had played its minor part in drawing them together.

"It's my choice," he answered.

She half reached for him, let her hand fall, and said, "I won't trouble you if you don't want me to."

He made a smile. "How could I not?" And in truth she was comely, brown and rounded, hair tumbling night-black past a face in which all the bloodlines of Earth seemed harmoniously mingled, her attire a wraparound skirt and a wreath of jasmine.

Her own smile flashed back at him. "That's better." Seriousness returned. He heard the concern in her. "But you're always lonely, aren't you? I mean inside yourself, where it counts."

"What else can I be, when I'm always among strangers?" he retorted without thinking. Immediately he wanted to protest that he hadn't expressed self-pity. But that could sound worse yet. He was too sparkbrained impulsive.

"No, we're your friends here!" she exclaimed, stricken. In some ways they were unreasonably vulnerable, these dwellers in mid-Pacific. Was it because they had scant contact with the rest of the world, or was it due to an obscure influence of the Keiki, those metamorphic seals, the other half of their society?

Certainly they had made him welcome, first as a visitor, then as a person who began to imagine he might pass his life among them. Boundless was the patience with which they forgave his gaucheries and explosions of bad temper, while teaching him mainly by example. He often wondered how much was natural kindness and how much was for the sake of his interesting foreignness, or even his verses.

"You and I—" Ianeke's voice trailed off.

"Yes," he must agree. She had gone beyond kindness, she honestly cared for *him*.

He could not break free of his mood. She regarded him with distress before she asked, "Were you making your new poem? I'm sorry if I interrupted. I'll go away and let you work." That too was genuine. Her culture made creativity an ideal, more powerful than he had found anywhere else.

He shook his head. "No, no, it's done."

Her eyes widened, then she bit her lip. "You sound displeased."

"I am. It's garbage."

"I can't believe that. You are too hard on yourself, *ipo*—dear one. How often have I told you? You are." She touched his hand. He felt and heard and saw the sympathy.

Sympathy! He nearly recoiled.

"There's nothing in it, nothing," he rasped.

"May I hear it?" She dared another smile. "Now is a good hour. You said the idea came at just this time, a few days ago."

"As you like." He took his eyes from her, staring above the Keiki Moana in their waves, and mumbled,

"The sunset throws a road across the sea,
Ephemeral as fire, with barely breath
Or ripple of a wrinkle on its bed,
Nor signs to tell the day, 'This way to death.'
They who descend past infra-violet,
Through that great night which underlies it, find
No quietness for silt that sank from life
To where the planetary millstones grind.
How will those ocean folk remember us?
How shall they and how can they? What we are
Has bones too thick to walk the western road
That smolders out beneath an eastern star."

"I do like," she said low.

He spat across the rail. "It's empty, I tell you! No sense of what I wanted to say—"

She moved to his side. "Of what is burning in you to say."

"Ha. The word for me is poetaster."

"No. You have the gift, you have the fire."

He shrugged. "Maybe, somewhere in my genome. What matter, when I don't have anything to use it for?"

"What do you mean?"

His fists knotted. "What I've been wandering the world in search of, and thought for a while I might have found here. The—the symbols and the substance." He drew a ragged breath. "Why has nothing new, nothing with real feeling in it, been done—in writing, music, every art, yes, every science—for centuries, I say, except by tiny enclaves like yours?"

"Why, Earth, Luna, Mars, they have thousands of fine writers—"

"Yes," rushed from him. "Brilliant persons turning out excellent variations on old forms, old themes, trying to bring something back to life that was worn-out before their grandparents were born. What's the sense in producing an imitation *Odyssey, The Trojan Women, Hamlet, The Waste Land, Elegy at Jupiter?*" His words gathered momentum. "Those spoke about love, strife, triumph, grief, terror, mystery, in the language of the people and their gods, or people who'd lost their gods but were gaining a universe. What life goes on today, except for what's been the same for longer than anybody has lived, the same safe round, now and forever?"

"I think we here—"

"Yes, yes. *You're* exploring, discovering, birthing new myths—" There flitted across him: In an offside corner of the planet, autonomous and undisturbed. But when someday those ways and dreams came forth into the

outer world, how troubling would they be to its peace? As
once the faith of Christ or Mahomet, the philosophy of
Locke or Jefferson, the science of Newton or Darwin, or
certain verses—

"—and you sing of them," he cried. "God, how I envy
your bards! I hoped I could share—" He choked.

She held him close. "You can. You shall."

He slumped. "No. It's no use. I'm too outside."

She stepped back, taking both his hands in hers, and
captured his gaze. *"Kāohi mai 'oe,"* she said low. "Hold
fast. You can learn to belong among us."

"How can I, when—when—"

As if to finish Nicol's question for him and be the answer to it, Tawiri appeared from behind the deckhouse.
To Nicol, the ship seemed to quiver beneath his tread.
Yet he moved softly, the muscles that sheathed his mass
under full control, cheerfulness on the round, smooth
face. "Aloha, Ianeke," he hailed in Awaiian. With the
help of an inductor, and still more the help of her, Nicol
had gained a fair command of the language. Tawiri gestured overside. The sun, become a red-gold shield, was
on the horizon. Glade blazed from it across the waters. "I
have been seeking you," Tawiri said. "We were going to
swim down the sunset road with the Keiki."

The young woman hesitated before she nodded. "Yes,
we were. I forgot. Jesse—"

Nicol knew he had the vigor to join them in the sea, but
not the style. What they intended was a dance, an art,
which they had started learning in childhood. Nor would
he ever fully understand what marvel it was they cele-
brated.

Bitterness rushed up in him, tasting of vomit. "Well, go!" he snapped. "Leave me alone."

Tears glimmered. "Jesse, I did not mean—"

He felt the rage as a tide that bore him forward, helpless. "Go, I said! Eject! That's an order!"

She lifted a hand to her lips, as if slapped. Tawiri flushed, scowled, and rumbled, "Belay. You should not speak so to her. To anyone." Incredulously: "And she your beloved."

"Mine?" Nicol yelled. "Everybody's!"

They stared at him. He sensed the horror in them. If Ianeke chose to share her bed with this friend also, what business was that of Nicol's? None, here or throughout most of the world. The fact that he loved her was irrelevant to everyone but him.

Tawiri hunched his shoulders. "That was *pupuka*," he said almost mildly. The word, not quite translatable, implied an appalling breach of decency. "You must redeem yourself." He meant performing an act of contrition before witnesses. Among the Lahui it was no humiliation. The usual aftermath was a feast, with much jollity.

To Nicol, in his condition, it was impossible. A fraction of him knew how crazy he was being, but had no power to brake him. "I'll redeem you, you smug slimeworm!" His fist slammed into Tawiri's stomach.

The big man lurched back, astounded, breath gusting from his mouth. He recovered and reached to grapple. Nicol had studied martial arts. Sometimes a contest worked some gall out of him. His response was equally reflexive, a sweep of legs and arms. Tawiri thudded down on the deck.

He sat up but did not rise. His glance raked the for-
eigner, as did Ianeke's. For a long while they were silent.
The sun dropped from sight, the sea-road faded into
darkness.

"I did not know this of you," Ianeke faltered at last.

Nicol looked away from them. "I didn't know it of myself," he forced, aware that he lied. Yet he had not wanted
it, he had not. "I'm . . . sorry."

"And we are."

Tawiri climbed to his feet. She moved to stand against
his comforting bulk.

"Yes," she sighed, "best you go. A flight touches at
Nauru, bound for Australia, tomorrow morning."

Where to, next? he wondered. Rage had drained away
and left him numb. Later, he knew, would come the remorse and pain. Now he felt only a leaden practicality.

A waxing half Moon shone pale above the deckhouse.
Maybe he should try his luck there. Why not? He could
do no worse than hitherto. Passage would consume most
of his small savings, and the cost of living would be
higher; if he didn't want to exist in poverty, he'd need
work, pay, to supplement citizen's credit. Well, he'd
heard about openings for Terrans in Lunarian outfits,
and Terrans from Earth were preferred—more physical
strength, ordinarily, plus the emotional factor of their
being outsiders, hirelings, rather than residents. He ought
quickly to acquire any necessary skills. Born and raised
in the Habitat, he was at ease with changeable weight,
Coriolis force, every trickiness of space. He'd gotten a
technic education as well, to learn how the modern world
operated. If, since then, he had become a drifter through

the byways of Earth, why, his knowledge should soon re-
vive. And if the Moondwellers were no more inspired or
inspiring to him than Earthlings, maybe their environs
would give him inhumanness to sing about, a latter-day
Jeffers. . . .

The thoughts blew past him cold and vague, like fog,
above a slowly congealing realization of what he had lost.

"But have it well, Jesse," Ianeke sobbed in Tawiri's
arms, "always well."

"And you," he said without tone. "All of you."

CHAPTER

Falaire lived in the Dizoune apartments among other Lunarians who could afford it. Hers fronted a corridor that at present gave the illusion of space; you walked through blackness, surrounded by frosty stars, between doorways limned by constellations.

At hers you entered a single great chamber, only the sanitor permanently hidden away. The floor, deep blue and yielding underfoot, extruded walls wherever she desired and reabsorbed them on command. From its half ellipse, sides curved nacreous to a ceiling vaulted and latticed, except where a section of native rock had been left unfinished. At the opposite end, a trumpet vine grew up a column to spread a canopy of leaves and fire-colored blossoms. Furniture, in the fine-drawn Lunarian style, was rather sparse; she liked room for pacing, dancing, or fencing practice. This evenwatch an outsize viewscreen had been set to generate a fantasy scene of towers reaching into a crimson sky where serpents flew on white wings. Music had dropped from savage passion to low and minor-key, sounds as of winds and strings, but with a subsonic beat for an erotic undertone.

She had enclosed her bed and left those mirroring surfaces in place when she emerged with Nicol. They had donned robes. Hers wrapped her closely in a sable that set off white skin and loose golden hair. They walked hand in hand to a table that her housekeeper had decked with a lacy cloth, a light repast, and a carafe of wine. "We will serve ourselves," she told it. The robot glided off to its station by the cuisinator and went motionless.

Ordinarily the humans might have stood, Lunarian wise in Lunar gravity, but Nicol was glad to indulge his relaxed body and sit down. Falaire did the same. At her gesture, he poured into the crystal goblets.

She lifted hers. *"Uwach yei,"* she murmured, traditional toast.

"Salud, amor, dinero, y tiempo para gozarlos." Still more ancient, Nicol's response suited the moment; but also, already, he felt a wish to declare his Terranness—his independence. Besides, she would jeer at a sycophant, perhaps most cruelly if he was a lover.

They drank, looking into each other's eyes. He thought, as often before, how he really knew nothing of what dwelt behind hers. In the past hour she had again revealed no more than an inventive enjoyment. The wine

was red and thick, pungently flavored. He didn't quite
like it, but best not say that. When he took a second
draught, it seemed less harsh, and warmth tingled
through his veins.

Falaire smiled. "Brood you again, so soon?"

Nicol shook himself. "I'm sorry. My mind wandered."

"Since you cannot in person? To wander is your nature."

Yes, she had come to know him in the times they were
together. In her embrace he had bared his wishes and
miseries; once he had wept. He tried for lightness. "I have
no wish to travel just now."

"Nor do I wish you begone." She took a salmon roe
wonton in her chopsticks and nibbled it. He thought of a
cat playing with a mouse. When she smiled, though, it
was reminiscently. "Those were some wondrous docking
maneuvers of yours."

"At a—a wondrous dock." He knew he was nothing
extraordinary in that regard. Well, she did lure forth
capabilities he had not suspected.

"I was reminded of your exploits in space," she said.
"Eyach, deft indeed."

"Not exploits. I never claimed—A couple of emergen-
cies, extravehicular operations, repairs," such as a
sophotect could have done more readily; but the main
reason for the Rayenn's existence was to keep some slight
human presence between the planets.

Why did his tongue flounder like this? Though he
wasn't glib, he could usually hold up his end of a conversation and handle a compliment without fuss.

"Now I believe those tales you told," she said.

"You didn't before?" He felt an irrational hurt. "You could have verified them, the reports are in the courai database—"

"Wai-ha, I teased. Be not so reactive."

"You are!" he flung back, and was immediately dismayed.

He had come to know the Lunarian look she gave him, and the inward withdrawal it warned of.

"I'm sorry," he repeated, the words stumbling in their haste. "No offense, querida. I only meant you—your people, they *are* fierce and—and mercurial, and proud." Proud as Lucifer, he thought out of books that few today knew.

Why was the afterglow of love draining from him this fast?

"We are not meek Terrans, nay," she said.

They ate and drank a while in silence. He wanted desperately to ease the strain he felt. Did she?

"I, I understand," he said at last. "I'm honored that you—"

She smiled anew and reached across the table to close fingers briefly over his hand. "You are not of the common ruck in your race. You too rage at your unfreedom."

"No, not really, not exactly." Try to keep things sane, he thought. Somehow he had come to the verge of an emotional eruption, his wits a-tumble.

Falaire raised her brows. "Nay? You have spoken of being born into a desert of the spirit."

"That's nothing I can blame anybody for." He must curb the quick, hot anger she evoked. It was absolutely not reasonable.

Her lips tightened, her tone went wintry. "I can and do. I curse this black hole of a world that sucks us in and crushes us formless. I would explode it if I could."

Yes, his mind continued for her, destroy it and then range adventuring, unhindered by economics. And reign a Selenarch, unencumbered with politics. Life a wild poem, ruthless as the *Iliad*, reckless as *Otterburn*. Beside that longing, his merely creative frustration was ludicrous. Yet his wrath seethed higher.

Falaire's laugh rang metallic. "Arai, who can burst asunder a black hole?"

Nicol groped for a way to diminish her bitterness and his, bring them back to their pleasure. "On Proserpina they're free." What she would call free.

"Who can escape a black hole?" she replied starkly.

"True—No more emigrant ships—" Few ships of any kind, anywhere in the inner Solar System, and nearly all of them altogether machine.

"Nor may yonder freedom last," Falaire said. "The cybercosm has decreed that they too shall be squeezed together into a little black-hole satellite."

"It's not that hopeless. Is it?" Was it?

Suddenly quiet, she answered, "It need not be."

He caught his breath. A chill shiver went through him.

She leaned forward. Her voice remained soft, but never had he seen or heard a higher intensity. "There are actions we can take, deeds we can do, even now, even now."

The knowledge flashed for a moment, that he was alarmed because a fragment of common sense told him he should be. "Hold on. You don't mean—Wait, the

Scaine Croi? Surely not. A, an exercise in futility."

Scorn retorted: "What know you of the Scaine Croi?"

"Why, uh, a resistance movement—" The name it gave itself meant The Knife Loose In The Sheath. "An underground, but, but what's the use?" Subversive propaganda privately circulated, which wasn't illegal. A few alleged acts of sabotage, a few alleged murders or other violences. Rumors of arsenals. Senseless.

"By being, it has kept our souls aflight," she said.

Yes, maybe that, he thought in his confusion. Affirmations, rites, mutual psychological support. . . . He didn't believe she indulged in such things much if at all, nor that anyone else did who still bore the old, aloof Selenarchic spirit. However, those Lunarians who in former times would have been their followers, knights and bailiffs and retainers, yes, those might draw nourishment from a secret society.

Nevertheless—"Action, though, did you say?" he protested. "Revolution? Guerrilla warfare? Insane!"

Once history was otherwise, he remembered. Had he lived before the cybercosm was omnipresent and omnipotent, he might have taken up a gun in some cause of his own.

Her coldness bit at him. "Think you I am stupid?"

"Of course not!" he cried. "I just don't see—"

She gazed beyond him and said low, "Through eons, a black hole shrivels away to naught. Rebellious particles quantum-tunnel out of it."

He realized abruptly and in full that she was not talking abstractions. He should have been shocked. Instead, a thrill coursed along his spine and out to the ends of his nerves. "You have . . . something under way."

Her look returned to hold him. "Yes. Dare you fare with me?"

"I can't—I don't know—"

"Dare you come hear what it is? You can refuse it."

And lose her. Clearly, she had invited him this time for this purpose. Had she ever had any other?

"Or you can help fire a shot for a freedom that will also be yours," she challenged.

It was crazy . . . lunatic. He must not let himself be borne along—on a swelling torrent of fury, of need to strike at something besides shadows—How was it happening?

Well, he could go listen. He must, or lose her here and now, and into the bargain know himself for less than a man. Mustn't he? What harm in listening?

"I c-can't promise, you understand," he stammered, "but, but, yes, I'll come."

Exultance flamed. She flowed erect. "Then let's be dressed and afoot. At once!"

CHAPTER
6

From his concealment Venator looked out into a room square-sided and bleakly functional. There was little furniture, but an array of sophisticated communications and computation equipment crowded it. A man sat before a screen, working a keyboard. He was caucasoid, of small stature, with a pinched yellowish face on a large head. In the three daycycles Venator had lain here, the man had not left the apartment, nor had earlier surveillance agents ever observed him. Food came in via robotic delivery tube according to orders entered at a local distributory. A brief visit by Lirion had conveyed the information that his name was Hench, he was an Intellect, and some kind of conspiracy was certainly going on.

The download's vantage point did not ordinarily let
him watch just what the dweller busied himself with. It
happened that now he could see. It was not helpful. A
screen displayed a chessframe, and he deduced that the
game was not simply three- but four-dimensional; the
pieces "matured" and "aged" with time. Hench was
playing against a computer. The rationale of the moves
on either side was beyond Venator's comprehension.

Two Lunarians entered. Lirion led, a scarlet gauze
cloak fluttering from his glitter-strewn blue tunic. Exultation lighted the stern old countenance. Venator recognized his companion from scenes clandestinely recorded
in the course of spying on him whenever possible. The
pair had met a few times, to go topside where no one
could listen in on them, and the other was readily identifi-
able—Seyant, nominally the lessor of these quarters, heir
to the modest remnant of a Selenarchic fortune, a peripa-
tetic and somewhat enigmatic young man. He was in
form-fitting black, with a broad belt of possibly natural
leather holding a large sheath knife. A habitual expression
of easy arrogance seemed now to be a hard-held mask for
his own excitement.

Hench looked at them, did not rise, but struck the can-
cellation key. His game blanked out of existence.

"You need not have done that," Lirion said. "You
could have put it on hold."

"Why?" Hench replied in Lunarian accented and
acrid. "It was pointless, except to fill in some empty
time."

Also meaningless, Venator thought. Even with an intelligence exceeding that of a Leonardo or an Einstein, he

must needs set the computer to play at his level; else it would have beaten him in perhaps a dozen moves.

"Will we get action tonight?" he demanded rather than asked.

Lirion nodded. "We should. Falaire has dispatched a signal to me. They will arrive shortly."

"At last."

"Have you the spaceship escape program ready?" Seyant snapped.

Hench bristled. "What else has there been for me to do but play with it?"

"You were to *work* with it."

Venator's mind leaped. Spaceship escape program. It must be for Lirion, but it could not mean that his craft would depart suddenly, without proper clearance. An Authority vessel would then be sure to go in pursuit, at higher acceleration than he could tolerate. No, Hench must have implanted a subtle distortion in the Traffic Control system, such that it would believe it knew everything it should—for instance, whether any passengers went along—but in fact let the ship go without collecting any real data. If Hench had been able to worm into the secrets of the cybercosm—no doubt remained that it was he and his equipment that had done so—then subverting routine procedures was no trick at all for him.

Lirion laughed. "Eyach, Seyant, hold your nastiness for when it's wanted."

"It is his specialty," Hench rasped.

"I would have this thing go as planned," Seyant answered sullenly. "We should have had one more rehearsal."

"You knew that what notice we got would be short," Lirion said. "She cannot program him as she would a robot."

Hench's lips twisted in a grin. "Besides," he remarked, "what we play this evenwatch won't be a scripted drama, it will be *commedia dell'arte.*"

Venator recognized the archaic term. Did the Lunarians? How many would, out of humanity's billion and a half?

"We must hope you have the wit to carry your role," Hench said to Seyant.

"Keep your quarrels for afterward, I tell you," Lirion ordered. "This will be flickery enough at best."

"I will not fail," Seyant told Hench. "If you do, if the ship does not get clear, then you will soon be dead."

"Nay," Lirion said. "Whatever happens, I forbid that."

"You are wise, captain," Hench said. "Only a dolt would break a tool because it got misused."

As often before, Venator wondered about him. How was he recruited for this venture? It must have been before Lirion arrived, although what Venator had heard last time strongly suggested the basic scheme was Lirion's, transmitted from Proserpina. The organization that made the arrangements was surely the Scaine Crói, which was Lunarian. It did have a few Terran adherents, for their own variety of reasons. But Hench scarcely counted as a Terran. He was a metamorph, an Intellect. The genome of his ancestors had been modified to shape a brainpower that computers made obsolete even before sophotects with full awareness were developed.

Venator guessed that he, alienated from a civilization
that gave him no real purpose in life, had been drawn in
by the challenge, the chance to play a genuine game for
genuine stakes—against the cybercosmic security system.
It was clear that no organic intelligence less than his
would have been able to plan and program for the operation, then see it through. Obviously the plotters could not
employ a sophotect. Supposing that somehow they had
been able secretly to build one with the needful intellec-
tual capacity, they could never have kept it with them.
Once it came into contact with the system, it would betray them, for it would realize where it truly belonged.
Oh, Venator knew, he knew.

Lirion addressed Seyant: "Remember, be not too bla-
tant. Watch for my signal to quell yourself, lest we
overdo."

The other scowled, offended. "I understand. Have I
not already been working with him?"

With whom, wondered Venator, and how?

A trill sounded. Seyant stiffened, Hench gripped the
arms of his chair. The coolness of a skipper came upon
Lirion. "Admit them," he directed the door.

Two persons appeared. Venator did not know either
the spectacular Lunarian female or the lean Terran male.
She was altogether self-possessed. Sweat glistened on his
face.

Lirion laid hand on breast, Lunarian courtesy salute.
"Well beheld, my lady and donrai," he greeted.

The man grew taut at sight of Seyant, who eased off
and gave him a supercilious smile.

"Pilot Jesse Nicol, Captain Lirion of Proserpina,

Hench," said the woman, with appropriate stylized gestures. She must be Falaire, and Nicol and Seyant must have met previously. . . . Jesse Nicol. Not very many people used surnames anymore, in those subcultures that produced those few individuals who attained his rank. A possible clue to this one's background and personality. . . . He was clearly agitated, struggling to maintain a surface calm.

"I have heard of you as a spacefarer of high worth," Lirion said.

Nicol glanced at Falaire, who nodded. Doubtless that meant that, yes, she had told the Proserpinan about him. "Thank you. But, uh, I'm hardly a spacefarer at all, compared to you," he said. His Lunarian, grammatical though unidiomatic, came out with slightly exaggerated precision, as if he were drunk but didn't want to show it. That wasn't actually the case, however; Venator knew the signs. Maybe Nicol was just overexcited.

"It is not the distances traversed that matter." Lirion's smile was sardonic. "Hai, the sole problem they pose is how to avoid going quantum from boredom."

"But once you've gotten to—a new comet, say—"

"Yes, the unknowns can kill." Uncharted gravel swarms, crevasses hidden under frozen gas, quakes, eruptions, even in those cold regions; it must be like pioneer days in the inner System.

"Not quite the same thing as a task done a few thousand kilometers from home, which a machine could do better," Seyant drawled.

Nicol flared. "Do you pretend you've ever done either?"

"Hold," Falaire interrupted. "Seyant, be more mannerly. At least two of Pilot Nicol's tasks were in fact hard and dangerous."

"I would be glad to hear of your experiences," Lirion invited.

"Why?" Nicol growled. To Falaire: "All right, why did you bring me here?"

"It was indeed unwitful," Seyant said. "What made you imagine we could trust a loosemouth Earthbaby?"

Nicol flushed and tensed as if to lunge. Falaire laid a hand on his arm and he curbed himself. Trembling a little, he told her: "If you wanted me insulted, you needn't have taken me this far."

"No, Jesse, never that," she murmured. Louder: "Seyant, hold your jaw."

"Like the lady Falaire—and unlike too many Lunarians, I fear—I have no dislike of your race, Pilot Nicol," Lirion said. "It is not mine, but it brought mine into being, and in its time it wrought mightily." He gestured at Hench. "Our respected associate here hails from Earth."

Still belligerent, Nicol snapped, "What's this all about?"

"Your promise, Jesse," Falaire reminded him.

He swallowed. "Yes. Whatever I hear, I'll keep confidential—"

"Amazing, if true," Seyant remarked.

Nicol glared. "You make me wonder if I'll choose to hear it."

"You said you would," Falaire put in.

"Yes—but if it's something wrong—"

"It is not," Lirion assured. "No evil, no harm. Rather, a deliverance. Your name can live in history with Anson Guthrie's and Dagny Beynac's."

"Then why this God damn secrecy?" Nicol blurted in Anglo.

Lirion understood. "You shall hear." He sighed. "Would we might offer you proper hospitality. May it later be unbounded."

"I could , . . do with a drink." Harshly: "But get to the point."

"Observe his demeanor," Seyant said. "Does it suggest him reliable?"

Indeed, such brusqueness would be rude anywhere, Venator thought. Among Lunarians it approached the obscene. If Nicol had lived and worked on the Moon, he knew that. If it escaped his control now and then, he must be under a nearly unendurable intensity of emotion.

He jerked a thumb at Seyant's knife. "Scaine Croi, huh? Your badge. Your childish ego token."

Lirion frowned. "We are squandering time and strength alike." His voice softened. "Pilot Nicol, in the name of the universe wherein we both find our lives, I ask your patience. This first meeting need not hold you overly long. Thereafter you shall decide whether there will be more."

Falaire took Nicol by the hand and with her eyes. He breathed deep before he said, "Very well. Speak."

"Maychance you have perceived that Hench is an Intellect," Lirion began.

With a heavy attempt at affability, Nicol said to the metamorph, "If you"—not a sophotect or an interlinked cybersystem—"handle all this gear by yourself, you can't be anything else."

"Computers do most of the work, of course," Hench replied in pedantic fashion. "But they are strictly isolated."

"What's the purpose?"

"For me? A pleasure not otherwise attainable, in the thing and the doing."

"As can be yours, Pilot Nicol," Lirion said, "together with rich material reward."

"If he has the nerve," Seyant added, just loudly enough for Nicol to hear.

"Say on," the spaceman grated, "before I break that blatherbrain's snotful nose for him."

"Seyant, be silent," Falaire said. "Jesse, we need him too. Bear with that for our sake . . . and yours."

"Even for Earth's, maychance," Lirion added.

"How?" Nicol asked.

"You have seen on the news what my mission is, and that it fails." The dialogue that followed reiterated Proserpina's need and the Federation government's refusal.

"Why this denial?" Falaire cried. "It would cost them well-nigh naught, set against the wealth they command. And we have offered to trade for the stuff."

Nicol stared at her. "We?"

Her gaze met his in pride. "Yes, I am of the Scaine Croi, and the Scaine Croi sees the morrow of the race and someday the liberation of Luna as on Proserpina. It was I who thought you may be the means of our salvation."

"Which could also be your own," Lirion pursued. "I too inquire, why are we denied? None of the excuses but ring false. Nay, it is that the cybercosm thinks millennia ahead. It computes how a new civilization could rise to full power among the comets and reach out for the stars. Then would it lose control over the destiny it wills for itself and the universe. No longer could humans, all organic life, be confined, be kept—ai, ever so kindly—for pets—nay, not that relevant, but an incidental epiphenomenon. Rather than that, shall they not bring forth whatever it will be that they dream of by and for themselves?"

"Bad enough having Guthrie's colony at Alpha Centauri," Hench put in. "The cybercosm can hope it will perish when its planet does, in a few more centuries; or, at least, that its survivors never get any farther. At worst, those people will be many years' travel away. Proserpina is here in the Solar System. No, it won't pose a military threat, unless you count maintaining defenses against possible attack. Aggression would be ridiculous. But given an adequate energy source, it will be going its own ways, gaining its own potency, and—people on Earth, Luna, Mars will notice. They will begin to question the order of their world, the whole philosophical basis of its existence."

Nicol quivered. "I've sometimes thought—Go on."

"A final consignment of antimatter is a-space in its robotic ship, bound from Mercury for storage in orbit beyond Saturn," said Lirion slowly. "This is a high secret, of course, but Hench has uncovered it for us."

"We knew something of the kind must happen sometime." Falaire's voice rang. "Now is the time, and our last chance."

Nicol threw up his hands. "Wait! You can't—no—"

"Yes," Lirion answered like steel. "We propose to capture that cargo for Proserpina. To this end we need a spacefarer who is skilled and a Terran."

"You, Jesse," Falaire said.

"No," Nicol stammered, "hold on, you're dement."

"The scheme is well wrought," Lirion declared. "Agree to it, and you shall hear."

"Agree blind, to that? No! I tell you, *I'm* not dement."

He doth protest too much, methinks, Venator reflected. Yet he was in truth not witless, whatever the present state of his nerves and glands. He might well be tempted, yes, strongly tempted, but he would not likely fall.

Evidently Falaire was closely acquainted with him. How could she so have misgauged him?

"We'll make it safe for you," she urged. "None will ever know, save a few who will never forget."

"And then when we are all securely dead, the tale shall be set free, to your immortal glory," Lirion promised.

"What good's glory to a dead man?" Nicol flung back.

"Eyach, you shall have pay worthy of the emprise, and no suspicion will come nigh you," Falaire said. She paused. "Unless, for your reward, you choose to fare with us to Proserpina."

He gaped, bewildered. "Us? You mean you?"

She nodded. "I claim that recompense for my part in this."

"But how—"

"You shall learn every 'how' when you have sworn to us," Lirion said.

"And if I don't like it—No, impossible! And, and it's piracy you're talking of, the greatest crime since—Falaire, don't!" Nicol reached for her. She swayed aside.

"See, I told you he'd shriek and flap," Seyant jeered.

The breath rattled in Nicol's gullet. "You're asking me to—"

Falaire cut him off. "At the bare least," she said coldly, "you've sworn to me you'll keep silence, whatever you have heard, that we may seek someone else."

"Someone with manhood," Seyant tossed in.

"Shut your hatch or I'll shut it for you!" Nicol screamed back. To Falaire and Lirion: "I'm going now, before I kill that slimeworm."

Strange, his overreaction, Venator thought. Granted, he already hated Seyant, and the taunts this evenwatch seemed calculated. Nevertheless, a spaceman couldn't do his job without a cooler head than Nicol was showing. Somehow he'd gotten into a quite abnormal condition. And it must have come upon him unawares, or else he'd recognize it, allow for it, and handle himself a good deal better.

Ah-h-h. An idea began to grow in the download.

"You'll truly not dare it?" Falaire was asking.

"How can I? Oh, God," Nicol groaned, and for a moment buried face in hands. "I understand you, your wish, and I—I could wish too—" He looked up. *"No."*

"Then we have naught else to speak of," she said. "Depart."

Lirion raised a palm. "First swear silence before us."

Nicol gritted his teeth. "Silence about a, a conspiracy—"

"You gave me your word," Falaire said. "We ask only that you give it anew. I believe in your honor. I have pledged this with mine, to these my spirit brothers." Her voice lowered. "I will not leave Luna for a while yet, Jesse. Would you see me arrested? They will correct my thinking, Jesse, they will make me into something other than what I am, if I fail to kill myself."

Shaking and sobbing, Nicol got out, "All right, I'll swear your damned oath." His own voice, high and cracked, told how near hysteria he was.

"Upon the Knife," said Lirion.

Seyant glanced down at his belt. "Nay. It would defile my blade."

"The Knife, Seyant."

The young man heaved a sigh. "As you will. I can consecrate another afterward." He drew it and extended it to Nicol, who took it blindly, automatically.

Consecrate? wondered Venator. Seyant had used the Spanyó word. It was not a Lunarian term, scarcely even a Lunarian concept. What was going on? Playacting—

Nicol hadn't noticed. The weapon shook in his grasp.

"No need for that," Falaire was saying. "The steel is alloyed with its honor."

Seyant sneered. "Not after it's been in the hand of a eunuch."

Nicol shuddered. "I'll have to wash that hand of mine, pretty boy," he coughed, "till I've got the top layer of skin off. Stay clear of me after this, you hear? I'm warning you, stay clear."

"Ai, I will," Seyant laughed. "I'd not have you publicly wet your breeches."

Nicol spat at his feet. Seyant struck him across the mouth. Nicol howled, a sound inhuman, and stabbed.

Crimson spouted. The guard of the knife stood against Seyant's tunic. He staggered backward and collapsed in a tangle of limbs.

Lirion seized Nicol's arms from behind. Nicol fought him, then sagged, the color drained from his face. Lirion released him.

Falaire and Hench crouched over the body. Hench's fingers searched across lips and pulse. He looked up. "Dead," he stated.

"So easily?" Falaire whispered.

"A major blood vessel severed, I think. Massive internal hemorrhage."

"No, please no," Nicol mumbled. "Call for medics. Revival—"

Hench shook his big head. "It would take too long, when we've no way here to cool him. Substantial brain cell decay."

Falaire rose and made a sign. "He would not want to be what he would be after they restarted him," she said quietly. "Give him his peace."

None of this was right, Venator thought. But Nicol was shocked and stunned beyond reasoning about it. Tomorrow his memories of it would have blurred into nightmare.

"And the police would make inquiry," Falaire continued. "Our undertaking would come to light, our cause be lost. You, Jesse, do you wish for psychocorrection, inhibition laid into your mind like shackles, and an end to spacefaring or any other work you ever hoped for? Nay, let Seyant lie."

Lirion nodded. "It is done, and belike the blame was chiefly his. Let him not have died for naught."

Their attitude was convincingly Lunarian, Venator thought, *if* Seyant had not been pledge-bound to them.

Falaire took Nicol's arm. "Jesse," she said, "come home with me. We'll not forsake you."

"I have no obligation of vengeance," Lirion told him.

"And I have my fealty to a dear friend," she said. "Jesse, come."

He stumbled away with her.

When they were gone, Lirion stooped above the body and withdrew the knife. Venator saw how the guard clung, and then how the steel came back out of the hilt as Lirion pulled the weapon free. A few more drops of what looked like blood trickled after, luridly red.

"How fares he?" Lirion asked.

Hench shrugged. "He should regain consciousness in about an hour, I'd say. Best leave him as he is for a few minutes, then carry him to bed."

So the retractable blade had pierced just enough to inject a drug—neurostat, probably—that gave instant anesthesia and reduced respiration and heartbeat to a pretty good imitation of death. The whole thing was staged to ensnare Nicol. Yes, Venator thought, these were desperate and dangerous folk.

Tomorrow a tiny robot would scuttle up the shaft to check on him. He would signal that he wanted to be removed, and it would go summon a larger machine. With luck, Hench would again be alone here and not notice anything.

When the Peace Authority had seized the four, clues should radiate outward to others. The plot would be broken and, Venator expected, the heart torn out of the Scaine Croi.

No public sensation. Everything kept as discreet as possible. But a well-phrased confidential message to the Selenarchs of Proserpina should chasten them. Some among them might begin to think that, after all, membership in the World Federation had many advantages.

Lirion laid the knife on a desk. "Meanwhile," he said, "let me see to another bit of business."

He strode toward Venator's place and touched a hidden point. The wall slid back from the cabinet. He confronted a case, about the size of his head, lying on a shelf. Optics on stalks swiveled to focus on him.

He smiled. "As I thought," he said. "Good evenwatch, donrai."

CHAPTER
7

Some thirty hours and ten million kilometers out of Lunar orbit, *Verdea* ceased acceleration, swung southward widdershins, and resumed boost at the same one-sixth Terrestrial gravity. The maneuver took place so gently that those aboard had no need to harness themselves. Safety regulations required it nonetheless, but this ship hailed from Proserpina.

Standing in her recreation room, Nicol set the viewscreen before him to scan aft. Earth still outshone all stars, brilliant sapphire upon blackness, the Moon a speck of amber close by. It was as if the clarity of the sight pierced through to him and drove the last fog from his mind. He couldn't tell whether that was good. He had his full awareness back, but also his pain and fear.

The room seemed both a refuge and a prison. It was small, with a few chairs, a table, the wherewithal for electronic and manual games, database outlets for shows or music or books. No one had yet activated the bulkheads; they enclosed him in blank, pale gray. The gymnasium, larger, equipped to let him maintain muscle tone through a long low-weight voyage, was on the deck beneath.

He breathed an air cool and, at present, bearing a slight odor of newly cut grass. Ventilation went silently, like thrust and recycling and nearly everything else the ship did. He might have been all alone in the cosmos, until a light footfall brought his glance around.

Falaire came to stand before him. The blond hair spilled vivid over a darkly iridescent kimono. In the plain coverall given him, he felt more than ever foreign to her. How unfairly beautiful she was.

"Aou, Jesse," she greeted. Fingertips brushed across his wrist. It tingled in their wake. "Are you hale? You look less than joyous."

He swallowed. "Why not? I've been—gone—Nothing was really real—"

"It was by your agreement."

Yes, he recalled blurrily, he had accepted the . . . the drowsy syrup she offered, when they got back to her apartment in that terrible hour. He had been raving with grief over his deed, ready to call the police despite every pledge he had given, but she persuaded him that he must seek a chemical calm, and thereafter—"I was like a robot," he said. "I had no will or feelings of my own." His recollection of the time was hazed, like memory of the

whole evenwatch earlier. He kept little except knowledge
of the fact, that it had happened. Nor did he want more.

"It was needful to keep you thus, that you could pass
through the spaceport and ride the shuttle up to our ship
without maychance making a scene that would draw people's heed." Falaire smiled. "The final dose has faded
away, I see and am glad of."

He shook his head, a blind effort to cast off bewilder-
ment. "How did you get us aboard without the spaceport
itself noticing?"

She laughed. "Thank Hench for that. Lirion will explain later if you wish. Suffice for this moment, in the
knowledge of the cybercosm he departed as he arrived,
companionless. You are free, safe, with us."

"How long's it been?"

"Since we left Luna? A watch or two past a daycycle."

His reasoning mind gave him a slight relief by shoving
anxieties aside as it worked. "Hm, yes, you'd want to start
out with vectors for a direct return to Proserpina. Now
we're far enough that TrafCon radar won't be routinely
tracking us, and it'll scarcely keep any other detector on
us either. You can change course for your target."

"Eyach," she said warmly, "indeed you are awake
again, a pilot whose skill is in his very speech. It bodes
well."

He must not let her lull him. "How long till we arrive?"

"Travel time is about nineteen daycycles at this acceleration, with midpoint turnover. Add some time to that
because we'll be in free fall whenever you are working
outside. Maychance thirty daycycles altogether." She

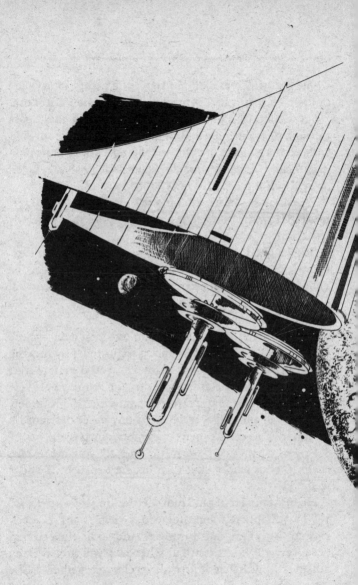

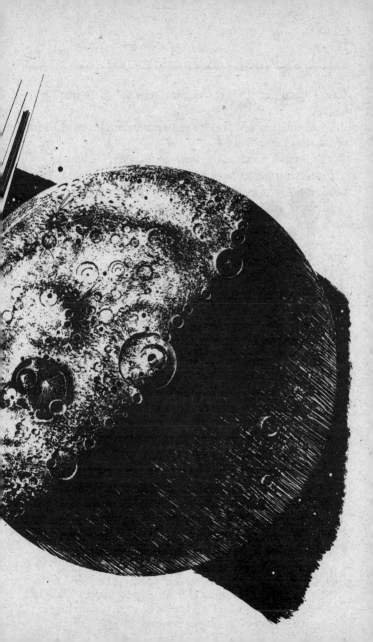

finger-shrugged. "Or thus Lirion tells me. I am but a passenger."

That was her reward, he remembered. Her reward for recruiting him. "And I—"

"You have become the hero of the tale."

Remorse rushed back to take him by the throat. "Oh, God, no!" he moaned in Anglo. "I'm a murderer."

She took his right hand, which had wielded the knife, in both hers. "Nay, Jesse. Think never so."

"I killed a man because—merely because he—What kind of animal am I?"

Her answer came grave and steady. "You are a man who, overstressed and overwrought, lashed out at what had waxed unendurable. Belike a different person would have had a threshold of tolerance more high. But we, Lirion and I, we bear you no grudge."

"You—he—I killed one of you, and, and me a Terran!"

"Heedless of race, Lunarians understand pride and honor."

Their kind of honor, Nicol thought amidst the turmoil.

"Seyant fell on his own misbehavior," Falaire continued. "I didn't like him anyhow."

Confusion redoubled. She didn't? Why, half his hatred had had its roots in jealousy. "But he was . . . at least he was your fellow in . . . the Scaine Croi."

The bright head nodded. "That much is true. You owe us, his spirit siblings—and, yes, his memory—a recompense. It shall be the part you take in our great venture."

The ugly word broke unbidden from his mouth: "Blackmail?"

She let go of his hand. Her tone grew severe. "Reflect

that you are in my personal debt also, for that I saved you from the consequences you would have brought on yourself. You babbled of needing punishment. But well you know it would have been worse than that. Psychocorrection. Neural alterations, re-education, elimination of your potential for violence. Your inmost self castrated, a poet and adventurer changed to a placidly contented citizen." Never had he heard such contempt as she threw into the last word.

His thoughts groped through shifting darknesses. Maybe she overstated the case. And yet—and yet—he was what he was. In certain ways he wished he were different, but the differences should be what he chose, and not go to the core of his being. "Well, but, but—"

"Unless that is your desire, then this escape is another debt laid on you. I claim it in the form of your service."

Silence fell. Nicol struggled. Now and then he gasped for air. He had won to a measure of calm by the time Lirion descended from the command center.

The old man wore youthful extravagance of scarlet, purple, and gold. "We are well on our course and the ship can run robotic," he declared, before he gave the Terran a close regard and added with a smile, "Aou, Pilot Nicol, welcome back to yourself."

"I'm not very happy about it," Nicol snapped.

Lirion made a dismissing gesture. "Eyach, yours is no abiding trouble. I heard what you and Falaire said." Was the vessel programmed for eavesdropping, Nicol wondered, or did an intercom simply happen to be on? "What guilt is yours you shall expiate, and go beyond it to become our moral creditor."

Guilt and atonement were not concepts that came

readily to a Lunarian, Nicol thought; and in fact Lirion had used the Anglo words.

"Not only shall you win forgiveness and overflowing thanks," the woman was assuring him, "rich material pay shall be yours. The funds are there on Luna."

Sarcasm awakened. "Precisely how shall I collect them?" he asked.

"That has been provided for," Lirion replied. "As Falaire told, your embarkation and hers with me was blocked out of entries the spaceport made in the general database. Your chiefs in the Rayenn—yes, they too are with the Scaine Croi—will record your absence as due to an assignment elsewhere, of no special interest to any authorities."

"Later they will likewise record my death and ashing in space," Falaire added, "for I am not returning."

"But as for you, Pilot Nicol," Lirion went on, "when your share of the mission is completed, this ship will double back to Juno and leave you there, before journeying home to Proserpina."

Nicol knew about that asteroid. It was among the few where some Lunarians lived, remnants of colonies formerly spread throughout the Belt, though today it was mainly a robotic control station and supply depot for what rare spacecraft still plied those lanes. "And then?"

"The Rayenn will dispatch a deep-space vessel"—of the two in its fleet—"to carry you back to Luna. There you shall receive your fortune, one million ucus, free and clear."

Astonished in spite of everything, Nicol exclaimed, "That much credit? How can I ever explain it?"

"Readily, if you are as wise as we deem you. A large gambling win, maychance. The police will not ask. If there is no reason to suspect crime, a change in some-one's personal account does not alert the system."

"I . . . suppose not." This wasn't the distant past he had read about, when government not only did not pro-vide citizen's credit, for people to choose what part of au-tomated production they wanted, but actually levied on earnings, among many other outrageous invasions.

Was the cybercosmic world so bad? Should he do this deed, this violation, against it?

"Thereafter," Lirion said, "you can live what life you wish."

"You can call up endless songs," Falaire murmured.

Bitterness rose into Nicol's gullet. "Maybe. If I can find anything to sing about." Or if Lirion didn't just kill him and toss the corpse into space. Simpler, safer, cheaper.

Her eyes sought his. "Might you rather come to Pros-erpina with me?"

However preposterous, the idea made his suspicions retreat. She seemed honest, if ever a Lunarian wholly was toward a Terran. And . . . these two were idealists, in their fashion—weren't they?

"Come," proposed Lirion, "let's go to the saloon, eat, take our ease, and rejoice together."

Falaire put her hand in Nicol's. He went along, sorrow already dwindling, excitement mounting. For better or worse, he was committed, wasn't he?

CHAPTER
8

After a gourmet luncheon and a siesta, Lirion showed Nicol through the ship.

Her hull resembled a squat, round-nosed cone, about three hundred meters long and as broad at base, studded with airlocks and housings, the thrust director of her drive projecting skeletal "beneath." Had you watched from outside when she was under boost, you would have seen just a faint bluish glow in the plasma hurled forth—unless you were directly aft, unprotected, within less than a thousand kilometers; then you would have been blinded, and very soon dead.

Inwardly, the forward half was divided by a succession of decks transverse to the acceleration vector. The first was barred to humans; that section held vital robotic apparatus, including the magnetohydrodynamic generator whose force screen warded off particle radiation. For added safety, the section behind it—below it, when boosting—contained storage lockers, auxiliary robots, and miscellaneous equipment. Next came the command center, where the captain received communications and data, and told the ship what to do; but usually no one need be present. A level of private cabins followed, then the deck for recreation room and saloon, which was also where humans generally entered and exited. Beyond/below lay the gymnasium, cuisinator, and assorted service modules. Past this in turn was the three-level cargo hold. You went between sections either by companionway or ascensor.

The after half was entirely off-limits to organic creatures. There were the gyroscopes for maneuver, together with much else essential, and beyond them the reaction-mass tanks, which doubled as shields against radiation from the motor. It was farthest back, antimatter trap, laser-electromagnetic pumps, fire chamber, plasma control, the powers of a mythic hell tamed and put to work.

Once vessels of this general design had been a familiar sight. But that was when humans flitted around the Solar System in great numbers. "On Proserpina they keep the wish to do their own spacefaring," Falaire had said. "But without ample energy to drive the ships, they must end huddled on their own worldlet, belike finally destroying themselves in wars brewed by life's emptiness, like the olden dwellers on Rapa Nui." Nicol had been surprised that she knew that obscure bit of Earth history. Of course, to her it cut near the bone.

Lirion stopped in the gymnasium, below the massive counterweight to the centrifuge's exercise platform, and said: "Before we go on, let us talk a while, to make sure you understand what you will see. Tell me about the ship we seek."

Taken aback, Nicol floundered, "M-m, well, I'd never given it any special thought till now. Why should I have?"

"Say forth, that I may correct you at need. Less peril lies in what you know not than in what you know that is not true."

"Agreed," Nicol acknowledged wryly. "Well—um—" He decided to begin more or less with the rudiments, to show that he too could be patronizing. "Antimatter is— was, this being the last consignment scheduled—it was produced on Mercury, captured according to Bose-Einstein quantum mechanics, and stored underground till a transport arrived. Then it'd be brought up and pumped into the ship by the same basic system which kept it confined—laser, electromagnetic—and refrozen as it emerged into stowage. Small ships delivered small loads to wherever they were wanted, Earth or Mars orbit, Luna, asteroids, outer-planet moons. The big ship, the one you must be after, took large loads out for storage in deep space. From time to time that reserve would be called upon, but in the past several decades it's mostly just been accumulating, till the government decided that no further production will be necessary or desirable for the next few centuries, if ever."

Lirion registered no offense. "Good, good. Where is that storage facility?"

"Who knows, except the cybercosm? In Solar orbit somewhere beyond Saturn"—hidden by sheer vastness—"that's all that's ever been made public. Only machines go there." Startled by a thought, Nicol peered at the lean face. "Have you learned where?"

"Yes," Lirion replied coolly.

"I don't . . . quite like that. Can any human be trusted with . . . access to the means of burning life off all Earth?"

"It matters not. The hoard is heavily guarded, by every sort of robotic weapon and a sophotectic intellect in watchful charge. No raider, no craft the least suspect, could come anywhere nigh without wrath consuming it." Lirion smiled. "I lack that ambition."

"Yes, I—I should have understood," Nicol apologized.

"It is the ship bound thither that shall be our prize. Tell me of it."

A flash of resentment overwhelmed prudence. *"Our* prize?"

"Say on," Lirion ordered.

Half helpless, Nicol yielded. "Well, uh, the ship's entirely robotic, though I suppose there's some kind of sophotect in it, probably inert but activated in any doubtful situation."

Lirion smiled again. "Shrewdly guessed. That is the case."

Soothed more than he believed he ought to be, Nicol proceeded: "It's public knowledge, has always been, the ship goes on a minimum-energy Hohmann orbit from Mercury to the depot, and back again for reloading. No hurry, no reason to waste fuel on boost along the way."

Lirion nodded. "Slightly less than eleven years, in either direction."

"You've gotten the exact figure?"

"Necessarily, since the orbit of the hoard is the prime secret. It circles the sun at approximately fifteen astronomical units of distance."

Nicol whistled, awed. Yet the cybercosm had more time and patience than mortals—cosmic time, machine patience.

After a moment, he ventured, "I'd assume the ship is armed too."

"Yes, against meteoroids. A serious impact is unlikely but not impossible, the sole hazard foreseeable"—Lirion chuckled, a low, purring sound—"hitherto. We cannot simply match velocities and lay alongside."

"I suppose not."

"Anything whatsoever that comes too close, or appears that it might, is to be destroyed, stone or ship."

Nicol nodded. "Y-yes, that does come back to me," among the things he heard as a child, a part of his education, but an incidental part, casually mentioned and presently forgotten. "Nobody has ever happened by like that, have they?"

"Nay. Secrecy and immensity have been sufficient shields, until now when we come with the knowledge to nullify them."

"You must have gotten highly detailed information."

"We did, through Hench. It includes the limitations of detectors and defenses. They are powerful"—the voice rang—"but not unconquerable, by those who have the skill and bravery."

Nicol waited.

"We can pass by at a distance of several thousand kilo-

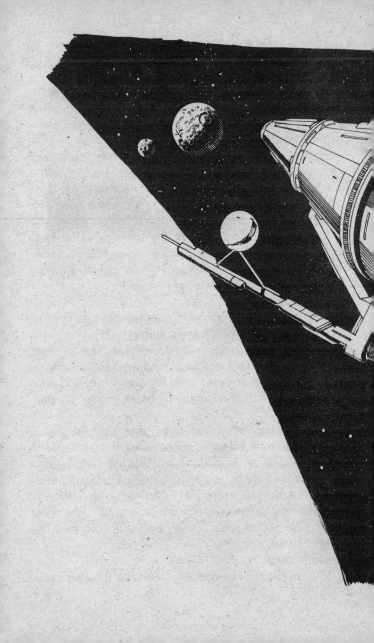

meters, on a trajectory that will bring us no closer, without exciting alarm," Lirion continued after a few seconds. "Such has been allowed for, as being bound to happen once or twice by chance in the course of centuries. But we—we will fire an energy beam to take out the ship's communications antenna. Suddenly it will be mute. It cannot tell its plight to the cybercosm."

And therefore no high-acceleration, sophotectic warcraft would set forth to retrieve and avenge, Nicol thought.

"The defenses will remain," Lirion said. "But they are intended for use against meteoroids, which have computable collision orbits. Yes, they can be turned on a spaceship that approaches too nigh. However, a small object moving at high and unpredictable varying accelerations, it should evade them."

The hair stood up over Nicol's body. "Ah-h-h," he whispered, "this is why you need me."

"Correct. You, with the adaptability of a conscious mind and the gravity tolerance of a Terran, can endure those stresses and arrive fit for action."

Despite all common sense and conscience, a thrill shot through Nicol. Challenge, risk, assertion of manhood against the machines!

"Once on the hull, you will take over the command turret." Lirion spoke almost dispassionately. "Thereafter the ship is ours. I will bring in *Verdea* and use her to start it toward Proserpina."

Logic nudged Nicol. "Wait," he protested. "Doesn't it make regular calls to Earth, verifying its position and that all's well? That's what I'd program."

"Indeed it does. We have a dummy ready to put in the Hohmann orbit, little more than a transmitter, which will give the proper signals at the proper intervals. Meanwhile the ship itself will come to Proserpina, years before it is due at the treasury."

Coldness waxed in Nicol. "What about the reaction when they realize? When the Teramind does?"

The answer was stark. "We will be prepared. But I do not expect the Federation to send a punitive expedition or missile barrage. Across yon reaches of space, it would be futile."

And the Teramind was above anything so human as anger, Nicol thought. Its long-range countermove—Who among mortals had the brain to imagine what that might be?

And yet . . . when the Proserpinans had gained this power, had crossed the energy threshold beyond which they would be free to grow without bounds: they would themselves be the unforeseeable factor, the randomness and chaos, that could perhaps thwart every profound calculation.

Maybe, maybe. Most likely no human alive had enough life span left to witness the outcome.

"In the daycycles ahead, we have much to do, making ready," Lirion said. "The instruments and weapons we carry must be taken out and emplaced, likewise the docking module whereby our prize is to be diverted. These tasks will require your strength and ability, Pilot Nicol. Moreover, you must learn your role, rehearse it, against every contingency, over and over. Eyach, you will be a-busied, you will earn your pay!"

Nicol tried to muster the resolution for he knew not what.

"Come," said Lirion in a milder tone, "let me give you a preliminary look at the gear."

They proceeded to the first hold. Its entry hatch lay inside a steel cylinder. Lirion took a three-centimeter disc from his beltpouch and applied it to the door. Nicol recognized it as an electronic key. Doubtless the lock responded to nothing else. The door slid open.

Lirion saw him observing and remarked, "This controls the locks to every compartment aboard. A precaution against possible . . . visitors . . . while *Verdea* was in Lunar orbit. Naturally, now most can be left unguarded." He grinned. "Should you wish privacy in any cabin, a simple closing off will serve."

The uppermost level held ordinary supplies and equipment. On the next deck down, the tour became very thorough, so much so that when they passed by a storage cabinet, Nicol asked, "What's in there?"

Lirion's response was unexpectedly sharp. "Naught of concern."

A quick, mutinous impulse made Nicol say, "Really? I thought I was to learn everything."

"Not altogether. It is of no concern to you, I say. Come along." Lirion lengthened his stride.

Nicol obeyed. His guide kept him too busy to dwell on the matter. Nevertheless wonderment lingered. What did the cabinet hide?

Hand weapons, he suspected, for just-in-case use—for instance, if he should become troublesome.

CHAPTER
9

Time and the ship passed onward through space. Nicol's waking hours went almost entirely to preparing himself. Sometimes, though, nature demanded he take a few of them off.

He lay with Falaire in her cabin. Like the others, it held little more than bed, washstand, closet, and computer terminal. However, she had activated the bulkheads. The moving, three-dimensional illusion of a forest that never was enclosed her and him. Trees rose out of night into a dappling, silvering radiance of clustered stars and a huge moon ringed with faceted diamonds. Feather fronds soughed to a breeze whose warmth bore odors like spice. The hueless light frosted her hair and limned her breasts above sliding shadows.

They had propped themselves up on pillows and been a while silent. Nicol stared into the dark. "Again you are troubled," Falaire said at last. ".You should not be," so soon after making love. Her tone and look were neither affronted nor scornful, as he might have expected of a Lunarian. They seemed half compassionate.

"I'm sorry," he answered. "I started thinking."

"You are ever thinking, nay?"

He shrugged. "Bad habit."

"Where went your thoughts this now?"

"Oh, never mind."

"But I care, Jesse." She laid her arm beneath his. "Tell me."

He doubted that she was quite sincere. How could she be? They were of two different species, and the fact that they could never bring a child into being meant less than the unlikeness of their psyches. At best, he believed, she was mildly fond of him. Of course, that meant he could hope to get his pay in money, not a bullet or a knife thrust.

Bitterness broke through: "The usual. What else?"

"That you slew Seyant? It plagues you yet?"

Speech became difficult. He found he was trying to say what he had been unable to, and had no chance to, before. "I . . . can't honestly be sorry he's dead—"

Falaire laughed low and stroked his cheek.

"But to know I'm a murderer, that's like a—a—" Groping, he seized on an archaic symbol. "—a cancer in me."

"I've told you over and over, you were overwrought and then he overstressed you."

"Who else will in the future?"

"Belike no one. You're intelligent, you learn your lessons. Besides, wealth should prove an excellent buffer against irritations."

"Will it? Are you sure? What can I *do* with it?"

"Whatever you choose that your Terran law allows, and I admit it is tolerant."

He could not help himself, he must turn his face to hers and demand, "Then why are you fleeing from it? What drives your Scaine Croi?"

He felt her stiffen. "Well you know," she replied curtly. "I said 'Terran law.' It is not for my race."

Nicol wondered why he so often wondered what her Lunarians wanted, and what it might in the course of centuries mean to his kind. Well, why not put the question? "All right, you're rebelling against the equilibrium society. But what would you make in its place for yourselves? What's calling you to Proserpina, Falaire?"—to be forever lost to him.

As he might lose a splendid sickness?

"I know not," she said. "There lies the greatness of it."

"But it can't just be chaos," he protested. Lunarians knew in their bones how unforgiving space was. "There's got to be some order, something—positive—"

"Eyach, yes," she breathed. "I was not very certain of it when we embarked. We hear too scantily from yonder." Nevertheless, she had embarked. Her voice strengthened. "But Lirion brought along not only vivifer scenes from Proserpina, such as you can play if you wish. He brought a dreambox program of life there. See you, he would be gone for many months, and this would relieve the barrenness of shipboard. Also, he foresaw the likelihood of one or two passengers coming back with him. From that program I have gained things I never quite had erstwhile, among them a clearer vision of my own desires." She paused. "Would you care to essay it?"

Astonished, he hesitated. "I, I have to spend most of my time with studies and simulations for the . . . hijacking, you realize."

"You can spare a bit. Indeed, I think it would be wise. To understand us better should hearten you the more."

He remained uncertain. A vivifer was one thing, presenting a show in several sensory modes like this image that surrounded him. A dreambox was not just interactive, it directly stimulated the brain. His nervous system would experience and record everything as real; afterward, nothing but his other memories and his reason would tell him it had been hallucinatory. He had seldom indulged, for he knew the temptation, the potential addictiveness, was high for restless, dissatisfied minds.

Probably that wouldn't be a danger in this case. The program had been prepared by and for Lunarians, aliens. But on that same account—

Falaire was watching him. The jeweled moonlight filled her big oblique eyes.

"Well—" He gulped. No, he would not be timid under that gaze. "Yes. Thank you."

Thus it came to pass that he sought the tank, disrobed, fitted on the helmet and associated connections, lay down in a fluid that smoothly changed its temperature and specific gravity to match his, slipped away toward sleep—

He floated in space. At his distance from Earth, the sun

was no more than the brightest of the stars. But they thronged heaven, and its bleak fierce luminance still equaled almost two full Lunas above Nauru. He could readily see Proserpina before him, and even trace out rills and ranges, darkling though the planetoid was.

Well-remembered science spoke to him. This was a piece from the core of a larger body that had orbited in what was now the Asteroid Belt, one of several fragmented by collisions over the eons. Jupiter had cast it into an enormous, eccentric new path, which passing stars drew higher yet. Some two thousand kilometers in diameter, it was chiefly nickel-iron with a stony crust; hence the surface gravity amounted to eighty-six percent of Luna's, ample for the colonists. Craters were few because impacts were rare in these immensities, but a comet had once crashed, bringing a wealth of ices and organics, and other comets were in range of venturesome spacecraft—and others beyond them, uncounted millions, the Oort Cloud reaching so far that its outer fringes mingled with the clouds around neighbor suns, an archipelago to lead multimillennial explorers ever onward. . . . Lights gleamed across the globe, the radio band seethed, humans lived here.

The ghost of Jesse Nicol flew downward, swept low above, beheld roads and rails, turrets and towers, domes, blockhouses, ground vehicles and space-suited striders, spacefields, the comings and goings of ships.

He went through an airlock and a tunnel to the country underground. For a short while he felt he was well-nigh home in Tychopolis, amidst slender arches, plazas where trees rustled to forced winds and fountains sprang singing, secretive doorways marked with kin emblems, small curious shops and worksteads—No. Those were Lunarians who walked the streets, quietly and alone or in aloof pairs or trios. At many heels or on many wrists and shoulders went a wild variety of metamorphic beasts, counter-colored leopard, miniature griffin, giant white bat, rainbow-winged hawk, feathered serpent. . . . Music trilled, soared, and throbbed on no Terrestrial scale. A troupe of dancers, masked and plumed, preceded a Selenarch and his lady. The ceiling high above simulated a violet sky where flames played in the clouds.

Ranging about, Nicol found that he had not actually visited a city. Proserpina had none, simply nodes of culture and commerce. Most folk lived apart, families by themselves or in communities that were feudal units, except that "feudal" was too Earthly a concept. It could be anyplace from a forested cavern to a topside castle. At intervals he glimpsed a Terran. Circumstances through the decades had brought a few here to stay. What was their life, they the tiny, foreign, childless minority? He didn't think Lunarians would deign to persecute them, but they were no part of the mainstream.

Their special abilities must be useful now and then in work for which robots were not adaptable enough. (If the Proserpinans had made sophotects at all, it was not evident, and any such machines were surely kept subordinate, their intelligence strictly limited.) Great engineering projects were under way, expansion of living space and capabilities, exploitation of resources, life overrunning this world and reaching out. They went with less noise and fuss than Terrans normally raised, but they went.

Nicol could, though, see how much more was needed, and how the work was beginning to starve for energy.

In heart-thudding eagerness, he set about sharing the life. He found he could not. It was Lunarian. When he tried to play an active role, the scenes dissolved into illogic and grotesquerie. The program could not accommodate him. He quit his efforts and became a passive, invisible observer.

He stood in taverns where captains returned from the comets related their odysseys. It was more than a quest for raw materials, it was shrewdness in the search and boldness in the seizing, it was danger—quakes, chasms, collapses, gravel storms, radiation leaks, equipment failures—and sometimes death, it was starlight aglisten on a mountain of ice sent tumbling toward Proserpina to become rain and rivers, it was comradeship (maybe more like a pride of lions than a band of Stone Age hunters) in striving and in victory. Wine splashed from crystal decanters, men and women flowed together. . . .

He watched a breakneck footrace over the thin-skinned crevasses of Iron Heath, a ceremony each year to honor the memory of Kaino, who first betrod it. (That was an Earth year; Proserpina's was nearly two million times as long, its seasons and the myths of its people cosmic.)

He saw a duel to the death, swords beneath stars till one blade ripped the other suit and water vapor gushed out, white, swiftly gone, an icon of the departing spirit. He observed how the families negotiated peace and how the celebration and the mourning were equally grim.

He attended a drama that was half a soaring ballet, and did not understand the conventions but sensed incandescent emotion. Nor did he understand what the wood-carver who sat on a mossy bank under a glass cliff was shaping, but somehow the curves and lines of it spoke to him. He heard songs—

After he left the dreambox, for the rest of that daycycle everything around him seemed unreal, a parade of flat puppets. Only a nightwatch in which he drugged himself to sleep restored him to what he supposed was sanity.

CHAPTER
10

Finally, finally the sessions ended, text, vivifer, simulators, practice; and actual work started. First Nicol brought out the guns, with their instruments, and installed them on the hull. Then came the docking module at the ship's nose, section by massive section. That was still more demanding.

Even so, as well schooled as he was, on top of his previous experience, the job proceeded rather smoothly. Robots did the bulk of the labor. He supervised, gave orders, made decisions, inspected and tested the results stage by stage, calibrated or adjusted, occasionally improvised, seldom exerted his full muscular strength. Often he need simply be present, aware of what went on but his mind free to wander.

Toward the end his musings began to take form, as complex molecules do in solution, their lesser units meeting randomly but making bonds according to the chemistry. There was no moment of revelation, yet there was a moment when he realized that something irreversible had taken place.

He stood on the hull, held fast by the magnetism his boots induced, a jetpack between his shoulders for when he must do more than walk from point to point, weightless because the ship went free on trajectory during these shifts. Sunlight had dwindled to a few percent of what fell on Luna, but his helmet must still darken to save his eyes whenever he happened to turn them that way. The matte surface shone mutedly, and shadows had slightly fuzzy edges. Illumination sufficed for ordinary purposes; otherwise, his suit carried assorted lamps to brighten a close view. Two robots scuttled like large beetles or stiff octopuses over the girders of the docking module, attaching the collar and the motors that would close it tight on the cargo ship's after assembly. With the sun at his back, Nicol saw them as if they moved across an abyss where stars beyond counting burned and the Milky Way cataracted frosty through silence.

Splendor, he thought. Here is the boundlessness out of which all things and anything may grow.

His gaze drifted south until he found Alpha Centauri in the multitude. Yonder are download Guthrie and the descendants of his followers, he thought. Doomed with their planet, or hopeful? We hear rumors of strange developments—only rumors, for communication was always thin across four and a third light-years, and eventually it ceased. Or so the cybercosm tells us.

No matter, I imagine. Unreachably remote. Such an exodus cannot happen again, at least not for a very long time to come and probably never. Proserpina, though, is here in the Solar System.

Barely. Guarded by distance, it goes its own ways. Given the wellspring of power—antimatter—what eerinesses will it bring forth, and what may they provoke on Earth? Unforeseeable, uncontrollable, chaos in the scientific sense of the word. No wonder if the cybercosm wants to curb it. The very Teramind is troubled.

Hu! A shudder. Best stay home among humans, my kind of humans.

What have they? Contentment, yes, peace, prosperity, but also adventure and achievement. For most people. Their doings may be old in history, but to each generation they are new, a dawn, a boat, a mountain, an ancient monument, a young sweetheart, enough.

Not for me, with my irrational, inchoate yearnings. For me, the passions will be in wild sports and wilder carousals, a play of lightnings above the ultimate void, until one way or another I kill myself and the void takes me back.

Stop that! Sniveling self-pity.

How ironic that this ship of fools bears the name of Verdea, the first Lunarian poet.

As for me, when I return home, what about a career in space? The task beneath my hands has been meaningful in its way, a difficult and not undangerous exercise in preparation for a desperate venture. And I have generally enjoyed serving the Rayenn. At rare, brief intervals the work became so intense that I *was* it. That is the ultimate, the sole true joy, to lose oneself in something greater than oneself.

But after this expedition, local spacehopping will be mighty pale stuff. Besides, I'd be unwise to stay on Luna. Clues just might link me to Seyant's death, if the Scaine Croi hasn't managed to pass it off as accidental. Or I might be blackmailed into aiding them again. No, better go back to Earth and let them forget me on the Moon. At night when it is in the sky I can look up, remembering.

Why was I that—dement—that *stupid?* How could I have been? Oh, I was subject to violent impulses all my life, and every so often they escaped my control, but never to this degree; and it did seem I'd fairly well mastered them. How else could I have trained for and held down the position of a space pilot?

True, Seyant was vermin—in my eyes—but that was no excuse. If only I could remember that evenwatch better. Why didn't I hit him with my fist? Well, but there the knife was in my hand; and there Falaire was, and he also her lover, or so she led me to think—

Nicol froze. He stood motionless until a synthetic voice in his sonors announced, "Unit B is now positioned and ready for you."

He shook himself, feeling he should do it as a dog shakes a rat, and went onto the girders. While he tested and fine-tuned, his body working as competently and almost as unconsciously as the robots, his mind flew to and fro.

I *cannot* be sure of the Lunarians. Maybe they mean to abide by their promises, maybe they don't. Certain is that they have been less than candid with me.

Have I any option but to go through with their piracy?

A weapon would give me some small leeway. Maybe

uselessly small, or maybe not what I would care to use. But at the moment I have none.

That forbidden cabinet—Bluebeard's chamber—Do Lunarians have a legend answering to Bluebeard?

It may or may not hold weapons. If not, at least I'll know I'm on an approximately equal footing with my shipmates, and feel more assured of Lirion's good faith. If he does keep concealed arms, then I want to be able to play the same game.

How to get into the cabinet?

Nicol began thinking.

CHAPTER

11

—————————————

—————————————

—————————————

Again the ship gave Lunar weight, decelerating, her bows pointed sunward.

Food aboard had been delicious throughout. Given a nanotechnic cuisinator, it had no reason not to be. Lirion had likewise been choosy about the drink he brought along. This evenwatch in the saloon, the meal was sumptuous, a festival. Brilliant patterns of light played in the bulkheads and music rollicked through jasmine-scented air. In Nicol's honor it was of Earth, ancient, Mozart's Horn Concerto No. 3.

Lirion raised his goblet. "The instruments and gauges declare you have done your work well, Pilot Nicol," he said.

Amazing how easy it was to dissemble. Nicol had never considered himself subtle. But then, the woman beside him and the man across from him were not of his civilization, not of his breed. Tones, expressions, body language—

"I'm less confident," he said regretfully.

"Ai, why thus?" asked Falaire.

"I'm not satisfied the installations will all be stable under heavy stress."

"They are designed for it," Lirion said.

"By Lunarians," Nicol replied. "With respect, your people aren't used to thinking in terms of high accelerations. I don't quite like the look of the docking module where it sits."

"An intuition?" Lirion scoffed.

"Grant me some sense for things like this, by heritage and experience. Listen." Nicol raised his forefinger. "We don't know exactly how the operation will go, except that we're bound to be improvising, and hastily. That could involve putting *Verdea* through evasive maneuvers at full thrust."

"True. We will be prepared for the contingency."

"But is the system, especially that module, as ready for it as you'll be? Could it do any harm to find out in advance of action?"

"What propose you?"

"I've given it thought and made estimates. We should program for about an hour at, say, one Earth gravity, followed by several quick turns and short boosts at up to three."

"Three Earth gravities!" Falaire exclaimed.

Nicol nodded. "Yes. Eighteen Lunar. It'll be hard on you two. But properly medicated, cushioned, harnessed, et cetera, you can take it without any real damage and soon recover."

Lirion frowned. "Shall we add that much time, including the revectoring afterward, before contact? It will be costly of fuel, too."

"Admittedly. But we'll need extra time anyway, if it turns out more work is required."

"And if it does not?" Falaire demanded softly.

"Then you'll have had your discomfort, even some pain, and the delay and all the rest—but not for nothing. We Terrans would call it insurance." They knew that concept, though in their society it was minor.

"M-m—" Lirion pondered. With the abrupt decisiveness of his race: "So be it."

Falaire caught Nicol's arm. "Truly you are one of us, Jesse," she breathed. When he glanced at her, her eyes gave promises.

He suppressed a twinge of conscience. After all, he was not planning to betray her, only to make as sure as he could that she would not betray him. "Let me explain specifically what I have in mind," he said.

CHAPTER
12
───────────
───────────
───────────

As he expected, the tests showed everything to be in good order. As he also expected, they left the Lunarians exhausted, hurting, and in need of much heavy sleep. He was somewhat tired and sore himself, but thrummingly alert.

Low weight and silence enclosed him. Cat-soft, his footsteps nonetheless seemed to racket in the passageways. Ease off, he thought, relax, or you'll be so clumsy you'll wake him, and what then?

The door to Lirion's cabin slid aside beneath his hand.

He had not been there before. Bulkheads set to a uniform, winter-cold gray, it might have been the cell of a medieval monk. Nicol felt surprised; or maybe he didn't.

The man lay stretched naked under a sheet, motionless save for the slow, deep breath. Grimness and mirth alike gone, he looked simply old. Compassion passed briefly through Nicol.

No time for that; but he dared not be hasty either, lest he make a clatter that would arouse.

He found the belt he sought, on a tunic in the closet, and drew the key from the pouch. Gripping it needlessly hard, he stole out.

Down the companionways, to the cylinder at the hold entry. Open it, open the portal within, climb on down through the first section. It was dimly lighted. Containers bulked like mythic trolls. Never had he felt more alone.

Next section. Turn on its illumination, white and chill. Cross a deck that reaches like an empty plain, now that most of what it bore is outside under the stars. Come to the cabinet and touch the key to its lock.

The door withdrew. Light spilled across a shelf at face level and, yes, two pistols. But it was the case that struck Nicol's perception like a hammer. Of dark-blue orgametal, a rounded box of slightly more volume than his head, it was set with connectors, sensors, a speaker, and two small hemispheres in front, about where a human's eyes would be. Within it, he knew, dwelt an awareness.

No. Not at this moment. The thing was clearly inactivated, the neural network dead. Nicol bit his lip. Wrong word, he thought crazily. Death did not mean the same to this entity as it did to him, nor did life.

Why was it here?

He didn't know how long he stood trying to think. It was as if the brain gyred within his skull. At last he realized he was shivering, and caught the reek of his sweat.

That was like a slap shocking him into purposefulness. An ally of Lirion's wouldn't have been shut away in the dark, would it? There didn't seem to be any alarm. He had come in search of truth.

Odd how steady his fingers were, pushing aside the appropriate cap on the box and reaching in to press the recessed main switch. At once he stepped back and stood wire-tense.

The front shells halved themselves and retracted. Two flexible stalks emerged, cups at their ends. They rose to their full length, fifteen centimeters, and swiveled slowly about. When they came to rest, they were aimed at him. Within the cups, he saw optic lenses gleam.

"Awake again—" The male voice spoke Anglo, with an accent from Earth's southeastern quadrant. It became a whipcrack: "Who are you? Is this a rescue?"

It can't attack me, Nicol thought, and it doesn't sound like a foe, and I'm starved for friends. He made thick tongue, dry mouth, constricted throat reply, "N-no, I, I don't think so—not yet—But what are *you?*"

The other spoke with machine self-command but human urgency: "Have we much time? What can we do?"

Nicol began regaining balance, as swiftly as men are apt to when crisis comes upon them. "Maybe an hour. Maybe more, but I'd rather not risk it. Speak low."

"We're aboard the Proserpinan ship, then?"

"Yes, bound for a rendezvous—Do you know?"

"Lirion told me in general terms." The voice turned impersonal. "He was willing to talk, being interested in how I'd respond, till he shut me off. We're bound for the boldest theft in history, the antimatter carrier, aren't we?"

"Yes. In two more daycycles."

The voice took on a hint of warmth. "I know you, Pilot Jesse Nicol, but you don't know me. Permit self-introduction. I commonly use the name Venator. I'm not a sophotect; I'm the download of a Peace Authority intelligence agent, revived when my service got wind of dangerous game afoot."

Nicol's flesh prickled as he noted the word "revived." More important was "Peace Authority." Ridiculous though it was, the sense of helpless isolation lifted a little from him, while the fear of being found out back on Earth gained strength. When Venator asked for his story, it rattled from him as if of itself, in broken pieces.

"But what happened to you?" he blurted.

Venator replied succinctly.

"Lirion's a crafty one," he finished. "The scheme was his from the beginning, with lesser inputs from fellow conspirators after he reached Luna—and from circumstances as he found them and took advantage of them. What an opponent! . . . He told me, there in the apartment, that at our previous meeting he'd guessed I'd attempt personally to spy on him. The layout invited it, especially since he was quick to remove safeguards that had been installed earlier."

The twists and turns left Nicol bewildered. "Do you mean he wanted you there?"

"Of course. Then my corps would assume matters were well in hand, and wouldn't strike at him in other ways."

"But now you've disappeared!"

"Hench was ready for that. Another distorted genius. He'd prepared an electronic deceptor. Maybe you haven't heard of such devices. When the minirobot came to check on me, it would get the sensor impression that I was still present and giving it no signal that I wished to be removed. Oh, yes, eventually my service will grow suspicious and raid the place, but by then all birds will have flown. They'll have left no particular spoor, thanks to what Hench planted in the TrafCon and security systems. Nor will the Authority be able to locate this ship, when she's deviated from her declared flight plan." Nicol nodded. Unless searchers had some idea of where to seek, immensity was a well-nigh perfect hideaway. "All they'll know, or surmise, is that Lirion completed whatever mischief he intended on Luna, or failed in it, and departed, presumably having discovered me and taken me along for interrogation and a hostage. Which, in fact, are his reasons. And they'll suppose that's why he's taking a roundabout way home."

"God, the gamble," Nicol whispered.

Venator fashioned a harsh laugh. "Lunarians are gamblers by nature, no? And this game of theirs was cannily planned and played. Also with you, my friend."

Nicol's throat tightened anew. "I've wondered—"

"Have you wondered enough?" Venator snapped. "Do you understand what Falaire's part in it must have been?"

Sickness welled up. "Falaire?"

"She was brought into the plot by those persons Lirion contacted through quantum encryption while he was still en route. Her assignment was to find a Terran space pilot who could be recruited or entrapped. I rather imagine the exact procedure was her idea too, when she'd gotten to know you. The execution of it certainly was. Another formidable brain."

"What—do—you—mean?"

"You did not murder that obnoxious Seyant."

Through thunders, Nicol heard the explanation.

"You couldn't have been provoked to it, in your normal state," Venator continued. "Clearly, Falaire slipped a psychodrug into you. Exoridine-alpha, I'd guess, in something you ate or drank. She'd have taken a counter-agent beforehand. Even after that, it took manipulation, very skillful and quite heartless, to make you strike."

Silence followed.

When Nicol had his wits back and could speak, it was out of a great interior hollowness. "I see. Yes. It makes sense. It accounts for everything."

"You're not to blame," Venator told him gently. "Instead, you're the single person in the universe who can retrieve this whole disaster."

"How?"

"Why, you need only beam a call to Earth. If you could come here secretly, I imagine you can do that as well, unnoticed, somewhere along the line. The Authority will send combat-armed, high-boost ships. They may arrive after the antimatter vessel had been diverted toward Proserpina, but they'll recover and redirect it, once they know what to look for."

"And we? You and me?"

"If you get your message off soon, this ship won't have gotten too far away, either, for radar and neutrino detectors to track her. She'll be no match for theirs. Lirion will release us to the pursuit. The alternative will be destruction. He'll doubtless try to bargain for being let go, himself and Falaire, and possibly the service will decide it isn't worthwhile to attempt seizure. Sophotects are pragmatists. Nor will Lirion take revenge on you. Besides your exchange value, well, Lunarians may be cruel, but they aren't senselessly vindictive."

"No," Nicol mumbled. "Sometimes they're actually idealists."

Venator's voice sharpened. "Study some history, and you'll see how much wreckage, misery, and death was due to idealists. Earth is well rid of their sort."

Impulse grabbed Nicol, like his life and free will asserting themselves. "But why do you serve, Venator? Isn't that for *your* cause, your ideal?"

"You could say I serve the cause that logic and experience show is the cause of peace and decency." The tone softened. "But—oh, perhaps I owe you a bit of confession—I have been an avatar of the Teramind. I hope to go back to its Oneness. Then I, this little spark of existence that is I, will belong again to that which truly understands."

Nicol stood hushed for a spell, as is seemly in the presence of a faith transcending the world.

"I see," he murmured.

Venator reverted to the practical. "You've more reason than that to be on my side. When Lirion and I were alone, talking, he answered a question of mine very frankly. He wasn't, and I imagine he still isn't, sure whether he'll honor his commitment to you. If he leaves you off where you can get passage home, can you be trusted to keep quiet for nine years?"

"I should think so, if I took part in the theft after . . . killing a man." A crawling went through Nicol's skin.

"You might break down."

"But those arrangements with the Rayenn—and, and Falaire—"

"Yes, as far as I could tell, which isn't extremely far, they and she intend to keep the pledge to you. And perhaps Lirion will decide to take the risk, if only for the sake of their good opinion. But perhaps not. Once you're dead, who'll bother to punish him? Done is done."

As if to shove the idea away, Nicol countered, "What about you?"

"I have my private stake in this," the download admitted. "Lirion and his colleagues obviously won't send me back from Proserpina before the antimatter is in their"—another chuckle—"I won't say hands, but in their possession. And why should they at all? I have plenty of information about my corps that they'd find most useful in planning any future escapades. The methods of getting me to talk and making sure I tell the truth won't leave much in working condition."

Virtual hells.

"I'd hate to believe that of them," Nicol said.

The tone conjured up an image of phantom shoulders shrugging. "He didn't threaten me with it, only with years of detention, and perhaps he won't do it, but I'd rather not make the wager."

"Or I my wager," Nicol whispered.

"Exactly. Now, have we exchanged enough? Safest will

be to shut up shop here as fast as possible."

The man nodded.

"I suggest you take those sidearms, keep one hidden, and get rid of the other," Venator went on. "Lirion won't likely come inspect this cabinet. Why should he? But if you are caught acting against him and Falaire before the consequences are irrevocable, you'll be glad of a weapon."

"Yes." Nicol slipped the pistols under his belt. "Shall I leave you awake?"

"M-m, I do have many thoughts to think. But you don't know when you'll be back, do you? Best not."

Could sensory deprivation drive a download, too, mad?

"All right." Nicol reached for the switch.

"Good hunting," Venator said.

Nicol deactivated him, then closed and locked the door. In like fashion, he covered his traces throughout the return to Lirion's quarters. The Lunarian still lay blind with sleep. Nicol put the key back and went on to his own place.

There he could let go and tremble.

Not for too long, though. He must pull his nerves together, consider and comprehend what had happened, and plan what to do.

Odd, how quickly he arrived at his decision.

CHAPTER
13

Across two thousand kilometers, to unaided vision the carrier was no more than a star, lost in the cold horde. It had ceased to move among them; *Verdea* fell free on trajectory, paralleling its course at practically the same velocity. The sun still dominated these skies, a tiny blaze you dared not look near without protection, but its radiance had shrunk to less than two percent of what Earth and Luna knew. Some two years into its journey, the carrier had left the orbit of Jupiter behind it. Speed had dwindled away, though, on that long climb; almost nine more years remained to its destination beyond Saturn.

If ever it got there, Nicol thought.

When he magnified with his optics, the ship swelled to

a strange small moon, a hundred-meter spheroid shining metallic save for shadows cast by the flanges that ribbed it like meridians. At the forward "pole" a mast jutted from the dome of the command turret, crowned with sensory and communications antennae. Aft projected the cylindrical lattice that held, at its end, a fission power plant together with a docking facility for the booster that had launched this vessel from Mercury orbit and the booster that was to bring it to harbor upon arrival. Equatorially between, a reinforcing spiderweb of struts braced four long spars sticking straight out, each terminating in a jet motor that could be swiveled around for orientation maneuvers. A thin metal skin sheened across the whole web, a radiating surface for the refrigerators inside the hull.

When Nicol magnified further, he saw how the flanges were not simply added radiators. To several of them clung the emplacements of energy projectors and nuclear-tipped missiles.

Well, he had known that. He had studied the images Hench stole from the secret database, and had rehearsed in simulation, so grindingly often that now he went through his part like another machine. That was not necessarily a reassurance. His mind was too free to think about contingencies and about what would come after, if he succeeded and survived.

Lirion's voice rustled in his ears: "Three minutes. Are you ready?"

"I am," he answered.

"Fare fiercely," called Falaire. He had no reply to that.

Instead, he ran mentally through a final review of his outfit. Space-suited, he lay several meters from *Verdea* in his darter. He had found no better name to give the craft, designed and built for this one buccaneering; the Lunarian "catou" wasn't really translatable. Harnessed full-length to an acceleration couch that would turn to hold itself always beneath him, he kept hands on a control panel—though mostly it was the robotic systems that would perceive, compute, decide, and act, faster than flesh ever could—and looked out through a grid of curved bars; otherwise, his section was open to the sky. His helmet stuck into a larger one that, upon his orders, gave him whatever display, amplification, readout, or virtual reality he might want. A rack beside him held the tools and weapons he would need, unless he met some lethal surprise. Behind him stretched a ten-meter cylinder—motor, reaction mass, nozzles pointing along three axes to thrust him hard in any direction. The ensemble would have been ludicrous elsewhere. Here it was hawk-functional, until it had served its purpose; then it was expendable, to be left adrift in the deeps.

Not unlike him.

He did not see the energy gun flash on *Verdea*, nor the light-speed strike of the blade it unsheathed. He saw the mast on the carrier flare white-hot at one point, another, another—break into loose fragments—for a short while they sketched the thing they had been, until they began slowly tumbling apart, a ruck around the turret—the ship was stricken dumb—"*Go!*"

Ten gravities slammed Nicol backward. A red mist blurred his universe. Stepped-up oxygen flow stung his nostrils.

The boost stopped. It was as if he had fallen off a cliff.

A moment later it smote again, laterally. The swing-around of his couch dizzied him. And again and again. He was zigzagging, randomly though always with an inward-bound component, lest a lightning gun draw a bead on him.

White slenderness appeared in his view field, enhanced image of a missile. Evasion snatched brutally. The thing passed by at a distance of kilometers. He called up a look at *Verdea* and saw the Proserpinan slide across the stars, jet aglow. The carrier's armament was only against mete-oroids, controlled by robots programmed for nothing more tricky, but Lirion and Falaire weren't taking chances. Whatever seemed to be converging on them, they would dodge while their own battery disabled it.

A second missile shot by, hideously close. The blood drumming in Nicol's head gave an illusion that he heard the whistle and thunder of its passage.

Now the carrier was big before him. The couch faced him completely around as brake blast wakened. His heart sprang high, for he was closing in, he was under the defenses and safe from them.

Deceleration ended, he was in free fall, the couch pivoted him back through a half circle. Quick! Not to risk punching through the ship's hull to its terrible cargo, the darter would miss it by fifty meters and fly away on trajectory, inert. He touched the control that undid his harness and the control that swung back the grid. A third gesture unsecured the rack of gear. He clutched it in both arms and pushed with his feet.

For a minute the cosmos cartwheeled. He let the rack go while he operated his jetpack. Stabilized, he recovered the object and, with vast caution, moved toward the vessel. The last few meters he went free. Contact shocked up through boots and shins to rattle his jaw.

The boots took magnetic hold and he was there, aboard his prize.

The knowledge that he lived swept over him in a wave and left him dazed, half delirious, breath going in and out, heart slugging, wet and pungent with sweat, garlanded with the galaxy.

Sense returned. He looked about him. The hull curved away under his feet, smooth metal sharply shadowed. Right and left, flanges made high horizons. Behind him, the radiator disc bisected heaven. Ahead was an edge to sight, he could not discern the turret, but two pieces of the mast were visible above, drifting, flickering as they gyrated, like grotesque stiff comets.

How still it was. His pulse had slowed to a low surf, his breathing to a whisper. Microgravity made him almost immaterial, a wisp of dandelion fluff briefly settled before the wind sent it onward.

He felt detached from himself, an intellect calm and limpid, as if he had lately recovered from a high fever. It was interesting to consider what he had won.

A hundred tonnes of antihydrogen, frozen into a solid block at a temperature of less than one kelvin. That made a sphere about thirteen and a half meters across, supported in a larger sphere of ordinary matter which it must never touch. Diamagnetism induced by the currents in superconducting rings provided the force. This required the same cold as did the keeping of the ice. A paramagnetic refrigeration system provided it. The power for that, and for all else, came from the fission generator at the bottom of the afterstructure. No more was needed; once equilibrium had been established, energy requirements were modest. It was in the sensors and feedbacks maintaining the balance that the true achievement lay.

To aid them, the inner shell was surrounded by the big hull. The volume between held machinery and circuitry, but mostly it held coolant, bled off into space as necessary, and radiation shielding. Even at close to absolute zero, the antihydrogen ice gave off some atoms, and atoms of normal matter outgassed from the container. Also, in order not to perturb the magnetic levitation, the ship had no generator for a protective field against solar wind and cosmic rays. Thus a slight haze of gamma ray quanta and esoteric particles wavered around the cargo. The wastage must be kept as small as the laws of physics made possible. The proper destiny of antimatter was to feed the fires of technology.

Antimatter, negative protons, positive electrons, contrary spins, all mathematically equivalent to holes in the vacuum, and when they met with the kind of matter that nature knew, both went up in a blaze of energy, near-total conversion of mass, the ultimate power source.

A metaphor, Nicol thought. Let it stand for the civilization and the dreams of the Orthosphere, the cybercosm in its reach from the Teramind to the humblest robots, the humans who lived according to its logic—set against the multitudinous civilizations and dreams of the Heterosphere, from metamorphs and dissidents on Earth to the wild Lunarians of Proserpina, and on beyond to the stars—What when *they* could no longer escape each other but came to their final meeting? Annihilation, or transfiguration?

God! Here he stood sketching out a poem! He had work to do. His laughter at himself echoed shrill in his helmet.

First, the odd pistol. He had slipped it from beneath his tunic and behind the things in the rack, the last time he went down into *Verdea*'s hold and practiced being in the darter. He got it, drew back his arm, and flung. The object spun free, gleamed fitfully as it caught sunlight, and was gone into viewless emptiness. Now he had only one to be careful of.

Get going. Raise a foot, a single foot, breaking it loose from its grip with a minor effort. Bring it forward and down. Repeat with its mate. Take care to have a boot always planted. If your body, swaying virtually weightless, loses both holds, you will float up, a bubble of air and blood, spaceward bound. A snort of the jetpack will return you, of course, but that is awkward and (irrational, when the hull can withstand micrometeoroid impacts, but nightmares are real phenomena too) you want no chance of piercing through to the doomsday load.

The turret lifted over the worldlet rim. It was a transparent hemisphere crammed with robotics and instrumentation, brain of the ship. No, say ganglion, nerve center, for the ship was an automaton, like a gigantic insect . . . bearing what pollen into the future? . . . Nicol lowered the rack and activated its magnetic base. He reached for the cutting torch it held. The next stage of his crime was a forced entry.

Crime, or military operation? What difference, especially when he was a conscript? Or a mercenary?

Where the flange on his left curved smoothly down to the hull, just short of the turret, a shape came from behind it and marched toward him. It shone like the metal everywhere around. Four legs bore a tank equipped with a jetpack. Above, three meters tall, loomed a cylinder topped by a sensory globe. From it reached four arms, each with its specialized hand. Any was capable of taking him apart.

A service robot.

Nicol's helmet recognized an incoming signal on the general band and tuned to it. The voice he heard was female. He didn't know why, maybe happenstance, the range in which it was synthesized being arbitrary, but this gave the final ghastly touch of wrongness. "What is the trouble? Hold still, do not stir, but explain, or I shall have to destroy you. This vessel and its cargo are inviolable. The command supersedes all else. Hold still, do not stir, explain the situation, or I shall have to destroy you."

When something unprecedented happened, the ship wakened the sophotect lying in reserve, and it took charge.

Nicol slipped his rocket gun from the rack. The robot was very near. He fired. The missile leaped, trailing flame, and struck in a gout of smoke. Debris hailed. The robot halted, a ruin. Fragments went off into space, vanishing fireflies. Some of them ricocheted first.

And he had worried about a landing!

"You appear to be human," the sophotect cried in language after language. "Unquestionably, an intelligence directs you. Explain, explain, or be destroyed."

Poor innocent. But more robots might well be on their way. Nicol replaced the gun, took out the torch, and moved up to the turret.

Energy played. Hyalon fused and vaporized. Nicol cut away a segment and cast it aside. It bobbed off, clownishly wobbling. He entered.

The layout within was complex, not meant for mortals, but his preparations had made it so familiar that his hands moved with never a hesitation. Touch this switch, keyboard that command, slide back this panel, sever that cable, bypass, nullify, make himself the master. Three more robots arrived, but they were little scuttering things which he demolished with a rapid-fire rifle.

"You that do this, know that you are totally aberrant," the sophotect pleaded. "Desist. I have powerful machines to help me."

Probably two or three big ones were left. They might appear at any time. They could perhaps overrun him.

"I am acting under necessity," Nicol stalled. "It's to prevent a disaster."

Such as the expansion of sophotectic intelligence, awareness, humanity's mind-child, through the universe, until in multiple billions of years it *was* the universe? No, he would not allow second thoughts, they could slow him down fatally. If he did not go through with the plan, Lirion would ask him why. He had forged his own plan after he spoke with Venator. Now he must abide by it or die.

"Before my long-range sensors were blasted, they perceived another spacecraft. The responsibility presumably stems from it. Do you realize what potential for horror is here? Explain your actions."

"I'm sorry," Nicol mumbled. He had reached the node he wanted. His fingers pounced to shut consciousness off.

I haven't murdered you, he thought amidst the instruments. Not quite. You can be restored to function. You can be restored to the cybercosm. I'll argue for that. But will it make any difference to you? I'll never know. You are too alien. As I am.

Now he could go about his work at leisure and in peace.

When it was done, he put the weapons and the cutting torch back in the rack, lugged it well out onto the hull, and with a heave sent it off into space, where the pistol had disappeared. When his shipmates asked, he'd explain that the loss was accidental; a robot he'd believed was demolished had suddenly flailed its limbs in a last convulsion before going dead, and also cast itself adrift. They shouldn't care especially. There should be no further need for the equipment.

After the rack was gone from sight, he called to *Verdea*, "All finished and ready for you. Approach at will." His voice came flat as the fall of a stone.

No need to talk the Proserpinan in. Robots did the piloting better than he or Lirion would ever be able to. He watched the ship draw cautiously nigh until she went behind the curve of the carrier. A while afterward he felt the thud as she docked and made fast.

More words to and fro became necessary. Falaire went into space, a living relay satellite for them. Nicol, the lord of the antimatter carrier, manually worked the motors on the rim, aiming the hull as the computers directed him.

The proper direction that they calculated was for two

hours hence. At that point *Verdea* would commence thrust, forcing her captive onto a new and swifter trajectory. Given so much mass, as well as the need for care, acceleration would be low. However, at the end of about eighty hours she could detach. The treasure ship would be bound for her home port, making orbitfall five years hence.

Meanwhile Nicol had ample time to rejoin her. The keenness of battle had eroded from him and left the dullness of total exhaustion. Eighty hours? Let him sleep and sleep, wake to go to the sanitor and maybe eat and drink a bit, then sleep some more. His tomorrow could wait until he was ready to cope with it.

He left the turret, pushed off, and jetted into the open, where stars reached everywhere around him.

CHAPTER 14

Weight that was low for Lunarians felt more ghostly to an Earthling than no weight at all. It brought a peculiar dispassion upon Nicol, as if a part of him stood aside and watched the doings of strangers.

But he was not truly calm. Beneath the rationality that observed, judged, and calculated, there crouched an animal ready to spring. Every sense whetted, he saw the shifting colors in the saloon bulkheads, heard the sibilance of his feet on the deck, scented a pine odor and slight chill in the air, with renewed knife-edge sharpness. The hour was on hand that would settle whether he lived or died, and how.

Lirion, who had called this meeting, waited with Falaire. His arms were folded, his features unreadable, and he had dressed in plain gray. She contrasted, a low-cut dark-red gown clinging to her, hair loose over the bare white shoulders. They had not seated themselves. Nicol took stance across the table from them. "Well beheld," he greeted in their language.

"Are you rested and refreshed?" Falaire asked.

"Yes," he replied truthfully if perhaps misleadingly.

"Good," Lirion said. "The time is nigh, Pilot Nicol," when *Verdea* would disengage and accelerate either for Juno or Proserpina.

"What is your decision?" Falaire inquired. Her eyes never left him. They seemed elfishly big and luminous.

Though Nicol had no wish to temporize, he judged it was best to get the matter spelled out. "What would you have me do?"

"Have I not said it enough?"—not often, because Lunarians did not entreat, but more than once. "I'd have you come with us to our world, and abide."

Lirion nodded.

"It need not be a lonely life," Falaire urged.

Her idea of loneliness was not his, her race lacked the Terran drive for sociability; and he knew she would never be constant, and doubtless would eventually weary of him and dismiss him. Yet he believed that in her way she was sincere.

"Remember," Lirion added, "you would be paid more than on Luna, by at least the cost of the fuel you save us, and be safe from Federation law."

For my part in the piracy, Nicol thought; but I can explain how I was trapped into it. For the murder . . . which I did not commit.

"Do you think you'd be safe from me?" he replied, level-voiced. The fear was surely in them: What if he learned Seyant was still alive? Their gang must have taken precautions, which included seeing to it that he did not stay on Luna; but nothing was infallible.

"We trust you, Jesse," Falaire said low. Lirion stared at him like a cat.

"Could you trust me on Proserpina?" Nicol challenged.

He had never raised the question before. It shook them a little. "What mean you?" Falaire demanded.

"It can't not have occurred to you," he said. "Distance or no, it takes a very small wattage to call from there to Earth; and the cybercosm is always monitoring, on every band. I'd have five years to find a transmitter, or make one, and use it clandestinely."

"Jesse, nay! Why would you?"

"To reinstate myself in my civilization, if I found I can't stand yours. Or for revenge."

She shivered. "Revenge—"

His grin twisted upward. "Therefore, whichever way I go, from your viewpoint I'm preferably dead."

She half reached toward him. "That you would think that of—" her glance went across Lirion, who stood masked with silence—"of me." The hand dropped.

"Perhaps not of you, dear," Nicol said. To her companion, briskly: "Lirion, you're right, we're due for a serious talk." He reached under his tunic and drew out the pistol he had kept. "Please go below and bring Venator to our conference."

Breath hissed between teeth. "Don't leap," N warned. "I'm a fairly good shot, and I can jum

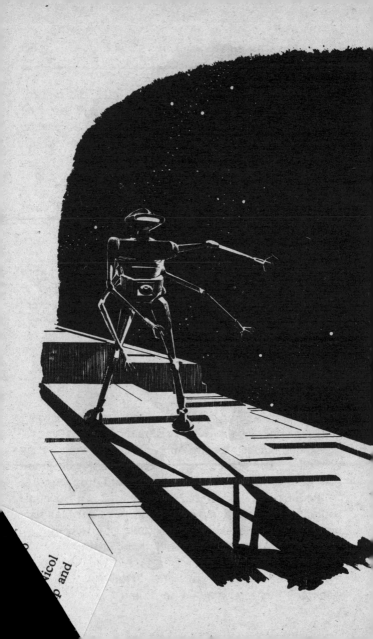

dodge better than you. Or you, Falaire." It hurt more than he had expected to say that last.

The Lunarians eased their bodies, as a snake uncoils. "I can guess what you have done," Lirion said without tone.

"Yes." Falaire's voice warmed. She actually smiled the least bit. "You are clever, Jesse, and bold."

"Thank you," he said. "Lirion, go."

The other man nodded and left.

Falaire softened further. He knew well what steel was beneath. "Are you death-angry with us?" she asked.

Nicol shook his head. "No. It's been like . . . an ancient war. Honorable enemies, insofar as honor was ever possible in war."

"A magnificent foeman, you. I had not imagined."

Did he hear lust, did she mean it, did she know whether she did?

"We have not harmed your Federation," she continued. "Should it desire more antimatter, there the plant is on Mercury. Another transport is easily built. Nor have we harmed you. Have we, truly? Whether on Earth or on Proserpina, you shall be rich, you shall have the means to live however you will."

"I'd like to make sure of that."

"Jesse, if you call Earth, if you dash from our lips this cup we have so sorely won—Ai—" The sound keened almost inaudibly. She did not weep, she did not plead. They poised mute, gazing at one another, until Lirion returned.

He carried Venator, already activated, and set the case down on the table before he took his place again by Falaire. "Say forth, Pilot Nicol," he snapped.

Eyestalks swung about, from person to person. "Would you please fill me in?" the download requested.

Falaire's look suggested she would like to fill him with concentrated sulfuric acid.

"The situation is obvious," Nicol said. "We've carried out the hijacking. We'll soon finish reorbiting the carrier."

"I see. Evidently you never got safe access to communications. Surprising." The synthetic tones quickened. "But now you're in charge. Good man, oh, excellent. I can promise you won't be penalized. On the contrary."

"What will you do?" Falaire asked.

"Lock you two away, contact Earth, and wait for the Authority," Venator answered. "What else?"

Falaire and Lirion considered Nicol, who stood motionless behind his weapon. "In truth?" she murmured after a while.

"I'm sorry," Nicol said to Venator. "No."

Jubilation flashed over Falaire. She curbed it and stayed watchful. "Ah-h-h," Lirion sighed.

"You realize I can't trust you," Nicol told them. "After everything you've done and everything that's at stake. And from time to time I'll have to sleep."

"Your danger from us depends on what your aim is," Falaire said.

"Not quite. Also, I'm putting an added price on my services, Venator."

"Why?" asked the download and the woman together. Eyestalks turned to meet eyes. His brief laughter barked, hers trilled.

"I don't want him . . . tortured, mutilated, dissected, scrapped—or kept forever from his Oneness," Nicol said. "No, I couldn't live with that."

Lirion finger-shrugged. "Eyach, we can readily cede you him, if what you further desire is what we need not die to prevent."

"It isn't. I do want to go to Proserpina with you, and, and live among you, your people—"

Falaire's cry of joy quivered for an instant.

"But you can't be sure of that, can you?" Nicol went on, largely to Lirion. "I might change my mind, on this voyage or in the years to come. And so I in my turn can't be sure of you."

"Unless you have an ally," Venator put in.

Nicol nodded. "Correct. You."

"Leagued with a criminal, a traitor?"

"Set those judgments aside. Think."

"Oh, I can do both. I see your strategy. If we stay together, standing watch and watch, it's not too likely we can be taken by surprise. In the end, when Proserpina has the antimatter secure beyond regaining, you'll arrange for my return to Earth."

"Yes. We need each other."

"A strong glue," Venator said wryly. "I have nothing to gain by refusing you. So to save myself, for whatever that may be worth, I, an officer of the Federation, shall be always at the side of a robber."

Even then, Falaire's grin flickered. *"Always?"*

In the depths of defeat, Venator kept his own humor. "Don't mind me," he said. "I'm only a consciousness in a box, indifferent to biology. At the appropriate moments

I can turn my optics elsewhere." He directed them toward Nicol. "The experience will admittedly be interesting. You're a complex devil. I think I'll enjoy your company. I hope mine doesn't become tedious to you."

"You need not forever be on guard," Lirion promised, perhaps honestly. "If you have not summoned Earth by the time we reach Proserpina, belike you never will."

"I'll keep trying to persuade him, you know," Venator said.

"Don't bother," Nicol told the download.

"What reason will we have to attack you?" Lirion argued.

"Yes, I daresay trust will come, however slowly," Nicol said.

"Maychance not too slowly," Falaire hinted.

"We'll see. For now, let's call this a truce." Nicol put the pistol in his belt, though he kept a hand near it.

Venator addressed him: "But I don't understand. I genuinely don't. Are you demented? Instead of a triumphant homecoming—justice done on this precious pair and their confederates, who deceived and used and all but broke you—or we could let them go, if you insist— you choose to give them their plunder and risk assassination, following them to exile. Do you know what it's like where you're bound? You'll be more foreign than any man ever was at the uttermost ends of Earth; and it's always night."

Nicol bit his lip. "I can't explain in so many words. Maybe as we get acquainted it'll become clear to you."

"Will you help me see?" Falaire asked most quietly. "For I too am bewildered, Jesse."

Lirion looked expectant. Given an idea of the space-farer's motive, he would know better what to await and thus be less inclined to plan some treachery. But Nicol spoke wholly to the woman.

"Yours is a new world, in a heroic age. Its bards are singing. I can hope to be one of them."

"You, a total outsider?" protested Venator.

Yes, Nicol thought, he knew full well how alone he would be; yet out of the pain he might win a meaning for his life. "Homer sang of a bygone age," he said. "Shake-speare treated of Cleopatra and Macbeth. Fitzgerald drew on Omar Khayyám. Kipling told about India. I—I don't even necessarily need human things. The inhuman may be what's mine, stars, comets, hugeness, a universe that doesn't know or care but simply and gloriously is—but humans are *there*—I realize it's crazy, and I can't ex-plain."

Venator spoke in sudden gentleness. "However, I think now I understand."

TOR
BOOKS The Best in Science Fiction

MOTHER OF STORMS • John Barnes
From one of the hottest new nanes in SF: a shattering epic of global catastrophe, virtual reality, and human courage, in the manner of *Lucifer's Hammer*, *Neuromancer*, and *The Forge of God*.

BEYOND THE GATE • Dave Wolverton
The insectoid dronons threaten to enslave the human race in the sequel to *The Golden Queen*.

TROUBLE AND HER FRIENDS • Melissa Scott
Lambda Award-winning cyberpunk SF adventure that the *Philadelphia Inquirer* called "provocative, well-written and thoroughly entertaining."

THE GATHERING FLAME • Debra Doyle and
James D. Macdonald
The Domina of Entibor obeys no law save her own.

WILDLIFE • James Patrick Kelly
"A brilliant evocation of future possibilities that establishes Kelly as a leading shaper of the genre."—*Booklist*

THE VOICES OF HEAVEN • Frederik Pohl
"A solid and engaging read from one of the genre's surest hands."—*Kirkus Reviews*

MOVING MARS • Greg Bear
The Nebula Award-winning novel of war between Earth and its colonists on Mars.

NEPTUNE CROSSING • Jeffrey A. Carver
"A roaring, cross-the-solar-system adventure of the first water."—Jack McDevitt

TOR
BOOKS The Best in Science Fiction

LIEGE-KILLER • Christopher Hinz
"*Liege-Killer* is a genuine page-turner, beautifully written and exciting from start to finish....Don't miss it."—*Locus*

HARVEST OF STARS • Poul Anderson
"A true masterpiece. An important work—not just of science fiction but of contemporary literature. Visionary and beautifully written, elegaic and transcendent, *Harvest of Stars* is the brightest star in Poul Anderson's constellation."
—Keith Ferrell, editor, *Omni*

FIREDANCE • Steven Barnes
SF adventure in 21st century California—by the co-author of *Beowulf's Children*.

ASH OCK • Christopher Hinz
"A well-handled science fiction thriller."—*Kirkus Reviews*

CALDÉ OF THE LONG SUN • Gene Wolfe
The third volume in the critically-acclaimed Book of the Long Sun.
"Dazzling."—*The New York Times*

OF TANGIBLE GHOSTS • L.E. Modesitt, Jr.
Ingenious alternate universe SF from the author of the *Recluce* fantasy series.

THE SHATTERED SPHERE • Roger MacBride Allen
The second book of the Hunted Earth continues the thrilling story that began in *The Ring of Charon*, a daringly original hard science fiction novel.

THE PRICE OF THE STARS • Debra Doyle and James D. Macdonald
Book One of the Mageworlds—the breakneck SF epic of the most brawling family in the human galaxy!